D0425153

# BOOK OF
# MOONS

**Also by Rosemary Edghill**

SPEAK DAGGERS TO HER

# BOOK OF MOONS

## A BAST MYSTERY

# Rosemary Edghill

A Tom Doherty Associates Book
New York

BOOK OF MOONS

Copyright © 1995 by Rosemary Edghill

This book is printed on acid-free paper.

A Forge Book
Published by Tom Doherty Associates, Inc.
175 Fifth Avenue
New York, N.Y. 10010

Forge® is a registered trademark of Tom Doherty Associates, Inc.

Library of Congress Cataloging-in-Publication Data

Edghill, Rosemary.
        Book of moons / Rosemary Edghill.
              p.      cm.
        "A Tom Doherty Associates book."
        ISBN 0-312-85605-9
        1. Women detectives—New York (N.Y.)—Fiction.   2. Occultism—New York (N.Y.)—Fiction.   I. Title.
        PS3555.D475B66      1995
        813'.54—dc20                                        95-34763
                                                                    CIP

First edition: November 1995

Printed in the United States of America

0 9 8 7 6 5 4 3 2 1

# Acknowledgments

A well-tuned mystery requires the author to gather together information of varying obscurity, which it is frequently impossible to do on one's own. Therefore I would like to thank (in more-or-less alphabetical order): Margot Adler, for reading this book in manuscript and offering her input, Greer Ilene Gilman, for tracking down Tom O'Bedlam in all his guises—and for the Morris Dancers (and thanks also to everyone in Greer's topic on GEnie's SFRT1—you were maahvelous), Greg Cox, demon editor, for not letting me get away with anything *but* murder, Myra Morales, for supplying translations into contemporary Spanish, Beth Nachison, for supplying translations into medieval French, Jennara Wenk, for the McGuffin (without which one cannot hunt tigers in Scotland). Any lapses, mistakes, and things of that nature must, however, be attributed to the author in their entirety.

All the spirits that stand with the Naked Man
In the Book of Moon defend ye

—"Tom O'Bedlam" (sixteenth-century ballad)

# BOOK OF MOONS

✠ ✠ ✠

# I

It was a Saturday in the middle of April and I was at the studio, making up for lost time at my day job by working overtime. I was short because last month I'd gone up to Rites of Spring, the Boston-area Pagan festival, and so had been out of the studio for more than a week.

Going to festivals affects everyone in different ways. It made me want to have a cleaner, larger, more upmarket apartment.

It made Belle want to have a similar festival here.

I suspected I was going to be asked to organize things, and I suspected I'd agree, because Belle and I were just now putting the icing on a patch-job of our friendship. It had been badly strained by the events of last summer and Belle's friendship was not something I was eager to lose, any more than I particularly wanted to leave Changing, which is my coven and Belle's.

The difference between us is that Lady Bellflower is Changing's High Priestess and I'm just another spear-carrying urban Witch. My name—my real name—is Bast, and you can stop doing that Elizabeth Montgomery impersonation right now.

Religion, Threat or Menace, is shaping up to be the hot issue of the nineties, as anyone who's studied the history of centuries ending in zero could predict. This time, however, the lines seem to be drawn not between this sect and that, but between those who believe in Deity—*any* deity, God or Goddess—and those who think that religion belongs in the past tense.

Wicca, the Religion of Witchcraft, the Old Religion, the Craft of the Wise, or whatever you want to call it, may be the new religion that sociologists and millenialists have been predicting since the 1950s—a life-affirming, politically correct, empowering, individuated, and nonsexist map to gnosis—or merely another post-Bomb, ante-millennial flash in the pan.

Personally my money's on the First Church of *Star Trek*, which has motivated more people in its various revivals than have ever heard of Wicca. This is why television is the religion of the masses, and religion is the television of the few, the proud, the freelance graphic artists.

Like me.

This particular Saturday I'd volunteered to take a rush job that Mikey Pontifex, our fearless owner, had dumped on Ray Lawrence (Houston Graphics' art director) at a quarter to five yesterday. The client needed it Monday morning by ten. Surprise.

Rush jobs with stupid deadlines are what Houston survives on, so it wasn't a question of whether we'd do it, but who'd get stuck with it. Ray has a wife and kid he likes to see occasionally. So guess who volunteered?

Besides, if I wasn't working, what would I do to keep out of trouble?

The phone rang.

"Bookie-Joint-Can-I-Help-You?" I sang into the mouthpiece, because Houston Graphics is only open from nine to five weekdays. After hours the studio is taken over by freelance graphic artists and other urban elves and, like much of New York, travels under an assumed name.

"Bast, is that you?" It was Glitter, a friend as well as being one of my coven mates.

"Sure," I said recklessly.

"It's gone," Glitter said agitatedly. "I've looked everywhere for it, and Goddess knows I didn't loan it to anyone; why would I loan it to anyone? And you've seen my apartment, Bast—I can't have overlooked it."

Glitter's apartment is bigger than mine, but not by much.

"*What* is gone?" I demanded, hideous possibilities suggesting themselves.

"My book," Glitter said, as if I should already know. "My Book of Shadows. It's *gone.*"

I tactfully stifled the urge to laugh, if only for sheer relief. "It's a mitzvah," I said. "Be happy." Which might have seemed callous, until you considered what Glitter's book looked like.

"*Bast!*" Glitter wailed in my ear.

I wasn't really worried yet. Dark forces stealing your Book of Shadows—BoS for short—is right up there with being under psychic attack by a black coven and being haunted by poltergeists as things that Do Not Happen In Real Life.

And besides, outside her day job, Glitter is not the world's most organized person.

"Did you look under your mattress?" I said.

There was a deep breath at the other end of the line. "I've looked everywhere. I've looked. I *have* looked."

"Okay," I said soothingly. "Have you told Belle?" Belle, being Glitter's High Priestess and mine, should logically be the first one approached with these little miseries.

"I called you first. Can't you do something?" Glitter said. "*You* know."

Whether it is because I have the misfortune to be a tall, blue-eyed, thirtysomething brunette who looks as if she has all the answers, or simply because I was born to stand in the wrong place at the wrong time, I am the sort of person whom people like Glitter ask to "do something."

Or it may be because last summer (if you believe the Magic Power of Witchcraft crowd—the ones who believe life is an episode of the *X-Files*) I single-handedly banished a black magician from the Community with the force of my immense Wiccan power.

He *was* a black magician. But he was hit by a car.

"I'm supposed to meet Beaner and go down to Lothlorien," I told Glitter. "But I'll come up after that, okay? I'll look for it for you."

I heard Glitter take a deep breath. "Okay, Bast. But it isn't *here*."

After promising to stop at the Chinese place on the corner and pick up two quarts of shrimp-fried rice on my way, I hung up. I stared sightlessly at myriad tiny veluxes of women in girdles. What I was working on, if I could believe the copy I'd run up in the front matter, was a source catalogue for fifties re-creationalists. The *nineteen*-fifties, you are to understand.

Next to that, *my* lifestyle almost looked mainstream.

I tried to believe that my recent phone call was some sort of a joke, but I couldn't convince myself that Glitter hadn't sounded serious. Still, I continued to hope she was mistaken.

A Book of Shadows is part logbook, part recipe book, part liturgy, and part magical diary. Every Witch makes her own out of material both handed down and self-created. It's a very personal thing, but on the other hand it wouldn't be that hard for Glitter to re-create the contents, even if she didn't have the help I knew that Belle would give her for the asking. The rituals in it are supposed to be secret, but that hasn't kept a number of different versions of the BoS from being published at one time or another, from *The Grimoire of Lady Sheba* on down through Raymond Buckland's numerous "Create Your Own" handbooks.

There wasn't much more I could do now, either about Glitter's Book or women in girdles. I tidied my area, took Friday's paycheck out of my purse, wrote "Karen Hightower" on the back with my Mars Technograph Number One, slipped it into an envelope for deposit to Chemical, and went to meet Beaner.

Houston Graphics is located (thanks to a long lease) in what used to be cheap commercial space in beau-

tiful downtown New York where Broadway meets La-
fayette—and for that matter, Houston.

It's still commercial, but it's no longer cheap. A
few blocks south the nabe remains authentically
tacky in all its antique sweatshop glory, but around
here the creeping Disneyfication of New York goes
on.

You could call it urban growth, but from here it
looks a lot more like a war; a war not against a gov-
ernment, but against an era. And, as in any war,
there are casualties.

In the Age of Fable, around the time I was learning to walk, New York was a city of bookstores. There
were the great uptown temples of Brentano's and
Scribner's, the lesser chapels like Shakespeare &
Co. and Gotham Book Mart, and no one had ever
heard of a national chain or a shopping mall.

Downtown was the Land of Cockaigne: used, secondhand, antique—call them what you like, they
were bookstores where you might, indeed, find anything. Stores where you would certainly find something. Sweet-smelling catacombs filled with second
chances for authors not fey enough to grab the brass
ring of literary immortality the first time out.

Economics and the rising price of real estate were
the Modred in this particular Camelot, and like all
good destroyers, they moved from the weak to the
strong. Today the Strand, at Broadway and Twelfth,
is the last faded standard-bearer of the thousand
shining emporia that once were threaded like pearls
on Broadway's shining silver cord. Scribner's,
though landmarked, isn't a bookstore anymore.

In the war against the written word, the logo-
clasts are winning.

* * *

It was raining when I got outside—that April rain with the subversive undertone of warmth that insists spring is just around the corner. I detoured to the ChemBank on the corner and sent my paycheck to join the other deposits. My boots splashed through puddles. A taxi cut close through the intersection, soaking me to my denimed knees. I caught up with Beaner under an awning near a coffee pushcart at Grand.

He tossed his Styrofoam espresso cup in the trash when he saw me and flung out his arms. He looked expensive and well kept, both of which he is.

"Bast! *Dah*-ling! You look *mah*-velous!" He also does the best Fernando Lamas imitation this side of Billy Crystal.

"Yeah. So do you." I hugged him. "How's it going?"

"We start full rehearsals next week." The rain had moderated itself to heavy mist. Beaner took my arm and we headed downtown.

From him I don't mind it. He tells me it's genetic. Beaner was born in Boston with a silver swizzle stick in his mouth to a family that is genteelly horrified at the path his life has taken.

His family doesn't mind that he's gay. They don't care if he's a Witch. What gives them fits is that A Son of Theirs is performing on the *public stage.* Which is another way of saying that Beaner is an operatic tenor and he does it for money.

This year he was abandoning LOOM temporarily—the Light Opera of Manhattan, if you're from out of town—for the Archival Opera Consortium, which was doing something by Donizetti called *Maria Stuarda.*

Which was why we were going to Lothlorien, a specialty bookstore (Things Celtic) that had survived Manhattan's misobiblic carnage through some oversight of the gods of urban renewal.

"And?" I said, because with Beaner the first sentence is never the whole story.

"Dearie, it's the usual. The soprano has a teeny substance abuse problem and a large attitude problem. Ken is a dear thing, but if we follow his blocking we'll all be impaled on pikes at the first exit. And then there's That Woman."

He shuddered dramatically and I laughed.

"That woman?" I asked, as I was meant to. "What woman?"

"Her," Beaner said. The distaste in his voice was suddenly real, not theatrical. "Mary. They're all raving Mariolators. I should have expected it, but if I have to hear one more person singing—you should pardon the expression—the praises of that round-heeled, dim-witted—"

"Mary? Bloody Mary Tudor?" I floundered.

Beaner stopped and patted my arm. "Mary *Stuart.* You should get out more, Bast, dear—and read some history that doesn't have Witches in it."

The rain had stopped and the sidewalks were fairly clear this far down. We began walking again. My elbow was left to its own devices.

"Mary Stuart." I sorted through my vast exposure to PBS miniseries and horrible movies that nevertheless contain the shining presence of Timothy Dalton. "Mary, Queen of Scots. Elizabeth's—"

*"Cousin,"* Beaner interrupted, before I could say

the wrong thing again. "Born 8 December, 1542, in Scotland, and a week later Papa died and she was Queen. Henry (that's the Eighth) wanted her for Edward, which would have been just perfect for England, but of course the Scots, oddly enough, did not wish to be an English province. So the adorable tot was smuggled off to France in 1548 and married Francis, heir to the French throne, in 1558. It must have been one hell of a Sweet Sixteen party. Widowed at the age of seventeen and went back to Scotland the same year—1560—where she ruled with such enormous ability that she was forced to run for her life eight years later," Beaner said. Venomously.

Maybe he was related to her travel agent.

"Anyway, she spent the next twenty years in an English prison as the centerpiece of plots formed by people who actually managed to be stupider than she was, and was executed in 1587, thank god."

I'm always impressed by people with a grasp of history that includes numbers. What I couldn't figure out was why Beaner was taking some bimbo who'd died before Boston was a city so personally.

"So she died four hundred years ago," I said.

"Four hundred eight," Beaner said promptly.

"You make it sound like she stepped out with your boyfriend last week."

"*My* boyfriends have much better taste," Beaner said, swanning it. We turned the corner and we were there.

"What the *hell?*" I said.

"Been awhile, has it?" Beaner said.

Lothlorien was in one of those buildings from the eighties—that's *1880s*—that aren't landmarked simply because New York can afford to squander them; a Victorian pseudo-classical riot of columns and friezes and pillars in cast terra-cotta and painted wrought iron, with skylights, pressed-tin ceilings, leaded glass, and strange rotundas.

But urban elves had indeed been busy while Bast was off having a life. The building's Victorian detailing, formerly a dirty green, was now picked out in *trés chic* colors of biscuit, terra-cotta, and teal. Brasswork glittered. Windows gleamed. There was a For Lease sign in an upper window.

"Good-bye Lothlorien," Beaner said gloomily. "The new owners are jumping Ilona's rent."

I skittered across the street, Beaner in pursuit, and rushed inside. Lothlorien was still there, for the moment. I released a breath I hadn't known I was holding.

Lothlorien Books inhabits a space that is sixty by ninety, with eighteen-foot ceilings. Around three sides are built-in shelves that go almost all the way up, with a ladder that slides along rollers and tracks for reaching the shelves and their contents.

It takes a visitor some time to realize how large the place actually is because every available space is crammed with books, both in single spies and in battalions. Lothlorien's specialty, as intimated, is Things Celtic: new and used, antique and rare, paperback and hardcover.

I inhaled the smell of books. There was a tape playing over the sound system, something wailing and fey; Lothlorien had recently started carrying tapes. Clannad, Phoenyx, The Chieftains. Things Celtic.

"Ilona!" Beaner caroled, stepping around me toward the counter. The subject of his salutation came ducking out from behind the curtain leading into the back room.

Ilona Saunders is an expatriate Brit, and the closest thing to a Grand Old Dame that the New York Wiccan and Pagan Community can boast. She's been running Lothlorien for at least forty years at the same location and has come to HallowFest every year for the last ten, despite all of which, she is tactful to the point that for all anyone knows she may not be a Pagan at all. She was wearing a print shirtwaist and a shawl held in place by a Celticwork brooch and looked like everyone's kindly old white-haired nanny.

"Can I help—? Oh, it's you, dear. Come for your tapes? I was just brewing up. Would either of you care for a cup of tea?"

We both declined, and Ilona vanished behind the curtain again. I looked around. "Tapes?" Beaner hadn't told me what his special order was.

"*Maria Stuarda,*" Beaner explained. "The Edinburgh Opera Received Version. One must do something."

Beaner leaned on the counter. I wandered around, looking at the new books. There were chairs for browsers, and most of the new stock was displayed on two vast oaken library tables in the center of the shop. I picked up a half dozen music tapes and a slipcased reproduction of *The Book of Kells* that I couldn't really afford.

"Here we are," Ilona said, coming out carrying a cup decorated with elaborate Celtic designs in stained-glass colors. She sat down behind the counter. I approached. On a shelf about eye level, an enormous brindled cat the color of the wood blinked green eyes at me.

"You look cheerful," Beaner said. "How's the moving going?"

"I've decided not to move," Ilona said firmly. "I shall buy the building and stay. What a pity I didn't think of it when Mr. Moskowitz was alive, but one doesn't, you know."

I glanced at Beaner. He looked bland, which meant he was stunned, and reasonably enough. To buy the building Lothlorien was in would cost a quarter million, minimum. How could a business like Lothlorien come up with that kind of financing?

"Come into money?" asked Beaner.

Ilona sighed. "Not precisely. I've decided to sell . . . Well, I suppose you'd call it an old family heirloom." She laughed a little sadly. "I admit it was hard to make up my mind, but I found I couldn't really bear to leave." She sipped her tea. "But you'll be wanting your order. Ned!" she called.

The cat blinked, slowly. The tape deck wailed about blood-red roses in someone's black silk hair. A person—probably Ned—appeared, descending the ladder that reached to the ceiling.

"Bring the special order for Mr. Challoner, will you, dear?" Ilona said, and Ned vanished in the direction of the back room. I formed a brief impression of dark hair and bulkiness.

"I don't know what I'd do without Ned," Ilona said. "I can't afford to pay him much—and if I'd sold up, where would he be?"

A silence fell. The next cut on the tape started;

drums first, then an eerie tangle of unaccompanied voices.

*"From the hag and hungry goblin / That into rags would rend ye,"* the singers wailed. *"All the spirits that stand by the Naked Man / In the Book of Moons defend ye—"*

"That woman again," Beaner said aggrievedly. "I'm being *haunted.*"

Fiddle and pennywhistle and drums that would make a dead man dance joined the singers.

"Mary, Queen of Scots?" I said. I couldn't see what she had to do with Mad Maudlin and Tom Rynosseros and the rest of Bedlam's bonnie boys.

"Oh, you know her?" Ilona said, as eagerly as if we'd just discovered a mutual friend.

"We've just met," I said.

" 'Tom O'Bedlam's a political ballad," Beaner said. "Sixteenth century."

Reasonable. Say something vicious, and, after enough time has passed, it becomes harmless art, suitable for children. Most of Mother Goose started out as political character assassination. Mary, Mary, quite contrary, how does your garden grow?

"And not a very nice one, either," Ilona said, just as if Beaner were making perfect sense. "Calling her a Bedlamite. Poor dear Mary—all she ever wanted was what was hers by right."

Ned came out of the back room with a glossy box that was probably Beaner's opera.

"Unfortunately," Beaner said waspishly, "what she thought was hers already belonged to other people."

I was looking at Ilona; Beaner wasn't. So I saw her

face go very still, the way a polite person's will when she has been mortally offended.

Beaner drew breath for another volley. I bumped into him, stepping on his foot, and set my purchases down on the counter. "Can you ring this up for me?" I said brightly.

"I can't take you anywhere," I said to Beaner. He sighed.

"My god, my god, I am heartily sorry for having offended Holy Mary Stuart, martyr of the True Religion, and never mind that since her son James the Sixth became James the First of England her cause was hardly lost. How was I to know that dear Ilona was one of *Them?* She's always seemed so sensible." Despite all the fluttering, I could tell that Beaner was flustered. He hates being *unintentionally* rude.

We walked uptown in the gathering dusk. The buildings were a mix of antique sweatshops, weird marginal industrial supply outlets, and newly remodeled buildings waiting for an influx of Pretty People. Probably they were owned by the same development corporation that currently owned Lothlorien's building and hoped to turn Lothlorien's space into a combination open-plan boutique and coffee bar, perhaps laying in a little neon around the plate-glass window to give the place just the right *soupçon* of cognitive dissonance.

Well, Ilona had scotched—pardon the reference— that notion. "Things Celtic, remember?" I said. Beaner shrugged, his opera under his arm.

"That reminds me," I said, to change the subject. "Have you seen Glitter's book?"

"Yes," Beaner camped, "isn't it *dreadful?*"

"It's missing," I said. He raised an eyebrow. "She says," I added.

"*How* could you miss it?" he demanded plaintively. He had a point. Glitter's Book of Shadows measures twelve by eighteen and is covered in purple metallic fabric decorated with sequins, rhinestones, and chrome studs.

"Anyway, I'm going to go up and help her look for it. You want to come?"

Beaner shuddered delicately. "Mary has any number of faults—but she is not fuchsia. Pass."

"Coward."

"Granted."

We parted at West Fourth, Beaner to a hot date with a dead queen and me to Glitter's.

Glitter lives on Dyckman near Broadway, almost as far uptown as Belle. The neighborhood was okay when she moved in to it a few years ago, but there have been so many "incidents" on her block since that everyone's nagging her to move. Even I am nagging her, which, when you consider where I live, will tell you how bad Glitter's neighborhood is.

She shrugs it off. I suppose you have a different view of things if you're a probation officer for the City of New York, which Glitter happens to be.

I picked up two quarts of shrimp fried rice at the Cuban-Chinese place on the corner and a six-pack of *cerveza fria* at the deli next door. Cold beer in hand, I headed for Glitter's building.

You can tell it used to be what New Yorkers call "a good building": marble steps, terrazzo floor. But it was a good building sometime around 1920—now it's just tatty. I buzzed Glitter's door first for courtesy, but her bell's been broken since she moved in, so I punched buttons at random and announced myself until someone let me in. Who knows?—maybe I knew them.

The building is six stories. Glitter is the top right front. There is a purple glitter star painted on her door that her fellow denizens have not yet been able to efface. I shifted my burden to get a hand free and knocked.

When Glitter answered the door I saw she'd been crying. I rearranged my mental picture of events: if not objectively serious (jury still out on that one), then serious to Glitter.

"Come in," she said forlornly.

"I brought beer."

"Yuch."

We sidled around each other in the narrow hall. Glitter locked the door. Rather than change places again, I preceded her into the apartment.

Kitchen downstage left. Bathroom on the right. Closet. At the end of the hall two tiny connecting rooms, about eight by ten each. Glitter uses the one overlooking the street for her bedroom, holding the opinion that when the world ends she wants to know it at the time.

I set the Chinese down on her kidney-shaped Lucite coffee table. Most of Glitter's furniture is transparent. She says she doesn't want anything interfering with the "full effect."

Glitter herself is part of the "full effect," so maybe she's got a point.

When I first met Glitter she wore large purple-tinted glasses, which have since been replaced with contacts that turn her eyes the color of drowned violets pickled in Welch's grape juice. She has her hair Cellophaned with Wild Orchid on an average of once a month, and there are very few items in her wardrobe that are not purple, or glittery, or both. Sometimes I wonder what her clients make of her.

"Glass?" she asked. I shook my head, extracted a Tsingtao from my six-pack, removed the cap, and drank.

"I'll get them," Glitter said, and bore the rest of the bottles off to her refrigerator. I looked around.

The walls—up to the strip of molding about eight feet up—were sponge-finished in fuchsia, purple, aqua, and just a hint of gold, all applied with the reckless disregard of the Manhattanite who knows she isn't going to get her security deposit back no matter what. The living room window shades were some paisley fabric, and the windows themselves were liberally swagged with cheap fringed gold shawls.

The three bookcases and the coffee table were all Lucite, as in transparent.

There used to be a Gothic Cabinet Craft–type place downtown on Broadway back in the early Eighties where you could get anything you wanted custom-built out of Lucite (including chests of drawers, but whose underwear is that decorative?). Glitter had patronized the establishment heavily.

I sat down on a throw pillow. Glitter came back with plates and chopsticks. I told her about Lothlorien's not-closing.

I was glad to see how much it cheered her up, but then I'd known it would. The rituals she designs for Changing have frequently been labeled the Celtic Twilight Zone. Like most people whose milk-tongue was Yiddish, the glottal stops of Gaelic are as nothing to her.

"Heirloom? What kind of heirloom?" Glitter wanted to know.

"An expensive one, I guess, if she's going to buy the building. She didn't say, and I could hardly ask, what with Beaner putting his foot in it big-time over Mary, Queen of Scots."

I watched Glitter closely for any signs of rabid partisanship, but she just snorted and helped herself to more rice.

After we finished eating, and I had another beer, we searched the entire apartment together. I did it because Glitter expected me to, and because to not do it would have been to call Glitter a deliberate liar. I was sure we'd turn it up in one of those out-of-the-way places that Glitter stashes things because they're so convenient.

But we didn't. It wasn't there. Not in the bedroom. Not on her altar, not under the bed, not stuffed behind the fabric swags concealing a horrible homegrown stucco job by the last tenant. Not in the bathroom. I even looked under the clawfoot tub. Not in the kitchen, although for a moment I entertained the theory that the roaches had decided to take up Wicca and stolen it. Not in the closet, although we did find a gorgeous pair of red silk stiletto-heeled pumps that Glitter couldn't remember buying and that were too narrow for me.

Not here. Not there. Not anywhere.

I sat back down in the living room on my pillow. Glitter swept her caftan around her and sat down opposite me.

Looking anxious. Looking as if she expected me to do something. "When was the last time you saw it?" I asked, giving up.

"This is—what? Saturday? Then Wednesday, because Dorje came over to copy the *Hymn to the Shopping Goddess* I wrote for when he goes to look for a new kitchen table," Glitter said.

One trouble our mainstream apologists have with Wicca is that parody is alive and well and living in the Craft. It's hard for the ethnography set to take us seriously when they're being told about New York Metropagan "Insta-traditions" like Etaoin Shrdlu rituals (useful if you're doing desktop publishing) and hymns to the Shopping Goddess (great for the urban scavenger). They forget that every liturgy was once written down for the first time, and that even Christianity used to have parody rituals and sacred clowns.

"Okay," I said carefully. "Is there any chance he took it with him?"

"Been there, done that," Glitter said. "I *called* him, Bast. He doesn't have it. It was here when he left."

Wednesday night. "Did anyone—"

"Break in? With my locks? And only steal my BoS?" Glitter jeered. I had to admit that she had a point. Despite the neighborhood she lives in, Glitter is careful about who knows she lives there and how easy it is to get into her apartment. If any of her current or former multiple-felony-commiting Probation Department clients ever managed to follow her home things could get messy.

"I thought maybe you could do a reading," Glitter said diffidently. "I got a new deck. I haven't used it yet."

"Sure," I said, since all magic aside, if a tarot reading would make Glitter feel better there was no reason for me not to do one. And besides, it wasn't as if I was going to charge her for it.

She came back with the reissue of the Coleman-Waite deck from the original plates that U.S. Games (the world's largest printer of tarot cards) came out with last spring. She set it down on the table and sat down across from me.

I shifted my pillow closer to the table and picked up the box. There is a great deal of ritual associated with reading the tarot cards, such as each reader having her own deck, wrapping the cards in red silk, and never letting someone else read with your cards. Even if you don't believe in magic, these rules focus your attention on the cards. You can't get serious help from something you take lightly.

Isn't paradox wonderful?

I broke the seal on the box and spilled the cards out. New decks are usually in order: first the Major Arcana, zero to twenty-one, then the fourteen cards of each of the four suits in numerical order, ending up with Page, Knight, Queen, King. I cut and shuffled and cut again until I was pretty sure that all the cards were completely mixed, then I set the deck down in front of Glitter and she cut it into three piles.

I prepared to do the reading that Glitter had asked for, based on the rules of divination as I knew them. What did both of us already know about Glitter's book that the cards would enable us to see?

Tarot, as I have said before, is a symbol system

that allows the unconscious and the conscious mind to communicate with each other—a language of symbol, invented to communicate something that has no language. Since many Witches believe that the unconscious mind is bound neither by time nor distance, it follows that it already "knows" the answers to most of the questions you may ask.

But—just like using your home computer—the art lies in getting it to cooperate.

I turned up the first card. A cloaked figure in a gray landscape, mourning over three spilled cups, oblivious to the two full cups behind him. Or her. The Five of Cups. Traditionally the card of not knowing what you've got, of swearing that your life is over when you still have *beaucoup* resources.

"Well, this much seems clear," I said to Glitter, holding up the card to her. She grimaced.

Like I said, on some level you already know everything you're going to find out in the average tarot reading. But the fact that Glitter could reconstruct her book from Belle's—as I interpreted the Five of Cups—was not a large amount of comfort when she didn't know how hers had vanished.

I laid out the rest of the cards. Wands: intuition, travel, the element of fire. Cups: emotion and the unconscious; water. Swords: logic, intellect, and the daylight mind; angels and aerials. Pentacles: Money, possessions, time, the Left-Hand Path, ruler of the things of Earth.

Overall, gibberish; a message I might be too close to Glitter to understand. I read tarot best when I have no stake in the outcome of the reading, and I didn't seem to be able to fall into that disinterested mode tonight.

I added cards and added cards until the entire tabletop was covered and I had the subtle but distinct impression that the cards were laughing at me (in fact there's one deck—Morgan's tarot—that has a card titled precisely that: *The Universe Is Laughing at You*).

I pulled the cards together and put the deck away. I looked at Glitter and shrugged.

"Call Belle," Glitter and I said in chorus.

Glitter unearthed her phone from a pile of cushions and dialed. In a few moments I was listening to a one-sided conversation—Glitter telling Belle she'd somehow sort of managed to slightly but permanently misplace her Book of Shadows, and could she make an appointment to copy a replacement out of Belle's?

Meanwhile, I considered my options vis-à-vis Glitter's information.

The book was not here. Fact. Dorje didn't have it. Fact. Glitter was telling the truth, as far as she knew it. Fact.

What did that leave? Nothing that made sense. Either someone had broken in without trace and stolen it and nothing else . . .

Or Glitter had lost it without knowing she had.

I considered that, looking around the room. It was not inside the apartment, but if she'd balanced it on an open window ledge and then bumped it, it *could* have fallen out, in which case it was gone forever.

But that was the only mundane, real-world possibility I could come up with, and it seemed a little far-fetched even for a charter member of the Conspiracy to Prevent Conspiracies, which I am.

"She wants to talk to you," Glitter said, waving a Louis XVI–style telephone receiver at me and derailing my train of thought.

"It's Belle," Bellflower told me, unnecessarily.

"Look, are you busy tomorrow night? I've got a candidate for Changing I want you to meet."

"Who referred her?" I asked. This was business as usual here on the New Aquarian Frontier. Belle usually called either Glitter or me to sit in when she was thinking of admitting someone new to Changing and wanted a second opinion, and usually me because I'm more or less out of the broom closet—unlike, say, Glitter, who might actually get into trouble if her religious affiliations (as opposed to her clothes sense) came to the attention of the City of New York.

At least as long as the *New York Post* spells "Wiccan" S-A-T-A-N-I-S-T.

"Him, not her," Belle said. "His name is Edward Skelton. He's been going to the Snake's Open Circles for a while. I talked to him on the phone Tuesday. He seems—" Belle shrugged eloquently down the phone line.

I knew what she meant. What can you tell about somebody's honest responses to the One True Polytheism (as some of us jestingly call it) from a few minutes on the phone and everybody on their best behavior?

And attendance at the city's most notorious occult bookstore's Open Pagan Circles might or might not be a recommendation, actually.

"Okay. When?" I said.

"Well, he wanted to get together on Wednesday, but Daffydd had night classes all last week and Edward works late hours three nights a week, so really the only time we could all get together soon was tomorrow."

"Sunday?" I mentally rearranged my notions of free time and sleeping late. But I wouldn't mind seeing Daffydd again.

Daffydd has another name when Columbia signs his paychecks. He's Belle's and Changing's on-and-off High Priest. She must be serious about this one if she was ringing him in, too. That, or she wanted backup for something else.

I had a hunch what it was, too. Beltane—May Day in the mundane world—was in two weeks, so if Belle wanted me to help her organize a Beltane festival, she was going to have to tap me for it soon. Like Sunday.

"Okay, Sunday's fine. Hunan Balcony down on 116th?" I said, guessing.

The Balcony is one of Belle's favorite neutral meeting spots, being right on the "A" line and not too far from Columbia.

"Sure. Seven o'clock." Belle hesitated, but if she wanted to talk about Glitter she certainly couldn't do it with her standing next to me. We said our goodbyes instead.

I hung up. I looked at Glitter. "New candidate," I said.

"That Skelton guy?" she said. I nodded. She shrugged. I didn't think anything of it at the time.

# 2

I finished the Nifty Fifties catalog up around noon Sunday and had a whole afternoon to kill before my dinner date appearance in my official capacity as judgment-caller and name-taker of the Wicca. I'd even dressed for the occasion, all in Urban Black: boots, jeans, turtleneck on one of its last outings before being packed away for the summer.

I wasn't alone in the studio, even if it was Sunday. Seiko was there, working on a project of her own. Seiko dresses like an all-night viewer of the S/M Shopping Channel, but the one time I dropped a few names from that area of reality I got nothing but a blank look. I can't think of any reason she'd feign ignorance while wearing all that leather, so I'm forced to the conclusion that Seiko wears chains and studs and leather because she *likes* wearing chains and studs and leather, and not for reasons of recreational athletics.

For what it's worth, Seiko is also the one who brought the Teenage Mutant Ninja lime Jello-O mold containing the secret ingredient of two bottles of vodka to the studio Christmas party last year. Ray recited all the verses of "Christmas Day in the Workhouse" and Mikey Pontifex actually smiled. It was a memorable occasion.

I packed up all thirty boards of the catalog up with the desktop page-for-page front and back matter (the catalog would run about fifty pages once a printer was done with it) and left it on Ray's desk so he could give it the Houston Graphics seal of approval when he got in tomorrow morning. I threw my used razor blades into the coffee can full of similar razor blades that I keep beside my desk and washed out my Number Triple Zero Mars Technograph and filled the reservoir with ammonia so that it would continue being a Number Triple Zero Mars Technograph pen and not, say, a cute and useless piece of modern sculpture, and even washed out my coffee cup.

Wasting time. If these were delaying tactics, my subconscious had a lousy sense of timing: the only appointment I could conceive of not wanting to go to was five hours in the future. I had all of Sunday afternoon before me. April in New York. The day was soggy and cool; raining again. You'll love New York, the ad campaign says. I put on my hat and coat and went out.

This hat was the latest in a series of hats: wide-brimmed black leather suggesting that I might be the biggest attitude case east of the Pecos. I like hats, but I never seem to be able to strike up a permanent relationship with one. But I keep hoping.

I didn't want to go home. Belle was off taping a week's worth of little recorded squibs for WBAI, and I felt too anticipatorily broke to want to spend money loitering in any of the innumerable cafés the Big Empty has to offer.

I had, in short, that rootless, disconnected feeling that comes of knowing there is a place you want to go, which for some reason you can't go to.

And as Katharine Hepburn always used to say, "Human nature, Mr. Alnut, is what we are put on this earth to rise above." So I squared mental shoulders (try it sometime) and headed for the Snake.

The Snake—also known as the Serpent's Truth—is on the northernmost fringe of the Village, on a street that't be a dead-end street if it weren't between Broadway and Sixth.

The Snake is, was, and always will be the kind of occult bookstore that makes the professional god-botherers' eyes light up in greedy anticipation. It is trashy, vulgar, tacky, and unabashedly commercial, with some of the highest markups for the sleaziest merchandise known to man or beast.

It also boasts a neon-purple industrial-strength chrome jukebox that contains every 45 that Elvis ever recorded. It is just too bad that among my many failings I can count an inability to listen to rockabilly in any form. Trismegistus, who owns both the Snake and the jukebox, knows this. He also maintains a Nietzschean faith in the perfectibility of humankind.

This is why, when he saw me coming up the street this particular afternoon, he dropped six quarters into the Mighty Wurlitzer's gaping neon violet maw and kicked the side. Elvis began telling me and everyone else within a two-block radius that he'd found a new place to dwell, with enough wof and yabber thrown in to make me hope that the speakers would explode.

Despite this encouragement, I persevered.

"Hi," I said to Tris, who, since he was loitering negligently against the jukebox, was also blocking my way into the Snake. Tris is not much seen in the Snake during the week, though where he goes and what he does no one knows. He keeps informed, though, and occasionally, in a truly heartwarming upswing of amateur standing over commercial instinct, Tris will ban someone from setting foot within the Snake's hallowed precincts for social crimes unspecified. I wondered if I'd somehow made it onto his blacklist.

"Howdy," Tris said after a moment, moving to let me by. I was reassured. I glanced downward and saw what I expected to.

The Boots. To be exact, bright red leather cowboy boots with snakeskin insets. Trismegistus, need it be said, has never been west of the Hudson in all his five decades, and has never been seen in any other footwear.

I rely for a certain amount of my mental equilibrium on intermittent sightings of the Boots, and in weaker moments have been known to fantasize the making of a perverse Nashville music video starring Moira Shearer and those boots.

Possibly my sense of humor is too obscure.

Having sidled into the Snake at last, I ran head-first into a palpable wall of Three Kings incense, which effectively insulated my sinuses from any other scent in the store. There was some slightly-older-than-New-Age tape dueling with Elvis over the antique sound system in the hope of encouraging the purchase of its brothers, and the narrow aisle that runs down one wall of this retail designer's nightmare and up the other was stuffed full of regulars, for whom a weekly pilgrimage to the Snake takes the place of a more conventional religious observance.

I inserted myself into their midst, a process not unlike that of a salmon's heading upstream to spawn. Safely wedged in among them, I looked back over my shoulder in the direction of the elevated platform that holds the cash register and felt a perverse jolt.

Julian was there. He was, as usual, wearing a Roman collar, a (probably) secondhand hammertail coat, and those tiny oval clerk's glasses. In my boots with two-inch heels I am about half an inch taller than he is, and I outweigh him by at least ten pounds. Makes a girl feel safe at night, superior strength does.

Julian, I hasten to add, had every right to be where he was, since he was the manager of the Serpent's Truth—aka the Snake—the man who ordered the books, the candles, the gen-U-wine Magus-Brand purple polyester acetate satin wizard robes, those commodities the sale of which kept the Snake in the black.

He was also the man who'd given my legal name and unlisted phone number to someone I would really have preferred not to have them.

This would have been a relatively minor crime, in the greater cosmic New York Metropolitan scheme of things, except for the fact that I had lusted after Julian and his tubercular seraphim good looks in unrequited silence for years, and to have him take just enough notice of me to sell me down the river was a betrayal on the supernaturally disproportionate order of the ones you experience in junior high.

Old scars are the rawest.

It was another reason I'd been avoiding the Snake. And the lowering grown-up consciousness that Julian had no idea what I'd managed to do to my psychic landscape with his (actually marginal) assistance did not make me feel one whit better, thank you very much.

So I buried myself in rapt contemplation of the Snake's antique herb collection, displayed in equally antique flint-glass jars all down the right-hand wall of the shop, and worked my way along the aisle, past the congested knot of browsers in front of the "Witchcraft and Women's Mysteries" section. The herbs had been new sometime around 1957. I didn't know about the jars.

Eventually I made it all the way down to Theosophy and Ancient Atlantis, which meant I was about as far from Julian as it was possible to get without going into the Snake's backroom ritual space. It also meant I was in a prime position to cruise the back-wall display of Santeria accessories.

I have no earthly need for a two-foot-high plaster polychrome statue of Saint Barbara (patroness of artillerymen and demolitions experts, a.k.a. the orisha Chango), but there's always the possibility I can talk myself into one someday. Besides, I was low on Uncrossing Floorwash and jar candles.

"I *trusted* you!"

Theatrical venom delivered in an undertone is always interesting. I opened my ears and turned sideways, as if my attention had suddenly been riveted by a four-volume boxed set of *The Secret Doctrine* and *Isis Unveiled.*

The dialogue was coming from the space in front

of the Santeria supplies. It's the largest open space in the shop—when Tris has someone here reading cards this is where the reader sets up her table.

"—*gave* it to you in good faith—" The speaker was doing a good job of keeping her voice down while filleting somebody fast and furious. I turned a little more and reached for one of the books.

"Xharina—" A man's voice this time. I almost dropped the book. I did look up. Xharina. Definitely Xharina.

Xharina—sometimes known as Xharina, Princess of Pain—is what you might call an ornament of the Community. Xharina runs an otherwise all-male coven in Brooklyn, and is a very decorative addition to any Pagan Festival, although not a real good advertisement for the Community at large.

I don't know what her day job is, and I don't want to know. I just wish I had the money she spends on boots, let alone the price of something like the laced-in little number she was wearing today, which looked like it had started life as a Victorian riding habit before it got its sleeves removed in order to display Xharina's full-glove tats to an admiring world.

At the moment the Princess looked like she wished she had the riding crop that went with the outfit. She was glaring up at the leatherboy who was probably one of her coveners—and, judging from the color of her complexion, wasn't going to be for much longer.

"I gave it to you to copy," she said in a low dangerous tone. "What do you mean, 'It's gone'?"

This was even more interesting than the admittedly interesting sight of Xharina. I could think of few things that one person would hand another to copy and get that bent out of shape at the loss of besides a Book of Shadows.

On the other hand, the boyfriend could have come up with a better place to tell her than the center ring at Gossip Central.

I sneaked another look around the end of Madame Blavatsky. Xharina was breathing in the jerky fashion of somebody who couldn't quite get enough air, and her Max Factor Sno-Pake was clearly outlined by the deep maroon of an approaching coronary.

"I just— I kept it safe, Xharina. I'd never—" The leatherboy's New York Nocturnal complexion was currently turning that shade of greenish white that is nearly impossible to fake.

"Just get it back," Xharina said. She turned her back on him and plowed through a knot of tourists as if they didn't exist.

More food for the legend.

She was moving too fast for me to catch her, and I wasn't sure what I'd say to her, anyway. I knew what she'd say, though, because it was what *I'd* say if some semistranger came up and asked *me* if my BoS'd gone for a walk.

Just like Glitter's.

I picked up a pamphlet on the Rollright Stones and tried to herd my wandering brain cells into some kind of order.

*If* I was placing the correct interpretation on what I'd just heard, Xharina had loaned her book to young Heather in Leather, from whose custody it had vanished.

It was, of course, possible that he'd gotten careless and lost it. It was also possible that the Pope would be marching in the gay rights parade come June.

Nothing else I did that afternoon was nearly as interesting.

I got to the Hunan Balcony on 116th a little before seven o'clock and spotted Edward Skelton instantly. He had that desperately eager air that was too intense for even the best blind date you ever wanted to go on, because Edward Skelton's blind date wasn't any mere corporeal bimbo, but Revealed Truth Herself.

He was also, I was pretty sure, Ned, the clerk at Lothlorien.

I needed a beer. I pushed open the door and headed for the PLEASE WAIT HERE TO BE SEATED sign.

Edward lunged to his feet instantly as I came in. It could have been the immense aura of witchy power that surrounded me, or, then again, it could have been the fact that you could smell the incense on my clothes from three feet away.

"Um, excuse me, are you . . ." he said, pushy and tentative all at once.

I felt an instant flare of irritation, and suppressed it because this is an awkward situation for anyone and he didn't need me to slam-dunk him on top of it.

"Reservation for a party of four," I said to the hostess who showed up about then, "under Flowers."

I turned back to Edward as the hostess began gathering up menus. "I think we're both waiting for Bellflower," I said with as much pleasant neutrality as I could muster. "Why don't you come on?"

We sat down. I ordered a Tsingtao. Edward looked surprised and ordered a Coke. I hoped he wasn't a better-living-through-dietary-fascism type, but even if he was, it wouldn't have much effect on either my life or the possibility of his inclusion in Changing.

He was here because he was looking for a coven to join, and because he'd either met someone who'd referred him to Belle or because of her show on WBAI. They'd talked on the phone a couple of times, and now Belle'd decided to let it go a step further. If Belle and Daffydd liked what they saw tonight, he'd be invited to one of Changing Coven's open meetings.

It's not much of an intake process, but it's all we have. You can't quantify sincerity—and sincerity alone isn't a virtue, anyway. The Craft, like all religions, deals in intangibles.

With that much settled, I took the opportunity to make a detailed survey of Edward Skelton, Wiccan-wannabe.

He looked like he was within hailing distance of thirty, but high or low I couldn't quite peg. I already knew that he was taller than I was. He had one of Per Aurum's medium pentacles on a leather cord around his neck and one of those big steel watches on his wrist that does everything but send a fax. A CZ stud in one ear. His hair was the darkest possible brown, a spiky buzz-cut that reminded me of porcupine quills or feathers, and his eyes were one of those extraordinary color combinations that hazel sometimes produces: a vivid green star around the pupil, the rest of the iris light brown with a dark rim.

But even with that promising beginning, something wasn't quite right. To this crucial meeting he had chosen to wear a white polyester short-sleeved shirt over a light green T bearing a design I couldn't quite make out through the translucent shirt. Blue jeans, dirty sneakers (when, as everyone knows, the current fashion is for dirty *work boots* instead). With that kind of fashion sense he was probably straight, not that it mattered to Belle, Changing, or me.

What mattered was that I didn't like him.

It was irrational; a telegram from the unconscious mind, swift and final.

We don't always get these flashes when they'd do us any good. Usually they arrive when they're an active social embarrassment, since, having made my mind up about Edward in the first five seconds of seeing him, I was reduced to playing devil's advocate to my better self for the rest of the evening, toting up items for the plus side of the ledger.

Our drinks came. I resisted the urge to order a second beer immediately. My day hadn't been *that* bad, and my night wouldn't be either.

"So. Have you known Bellflower long?" Edward said. "I'm Edward Skelton. Ned."

"Yeah," I said. "We've met."

"You were at the bookstore," Ned said, pleased with himself for remembering. I nodded, and was instantly irritated with myself for being so condescending.

Ned began to talk. He turned out to be one of those people who show up somewhere full of questions and then engage in a nonstop monologue about themselves. This was an unfair assessment, and I wrestled with my better nature while I consumed the first of what would be not-too-many Tsingtaos and learned that Ned was the youngest of four and the only boy, came from upstate New York, and had come to the City in the face of massive parental disapproval.

"They wanted me to be a doctor—my dad's a doctor—but I couldn't really see going through all that when what I wanted to do was write." He sipped his Coke. "I'm a writer, really."

In Manhattan we spell this word *unemployed*.

"Anything published?" I asked, although I could guess the answer.

Ned shrugged, embarrassed. "A couple of things. You know, like in magazines? Small press."

About then Daffydd and Belle arrived.

Daffydd is tall and spare and favors tweed jackets with black turtlenecks, giving him a passing resemblance to a member of a road show company of *Bell, Book, and Candle*. Other than a pentacle ring and his HP bracelet he looks absolutely mundane and very reassuring.

Daffydd's interest in the Craft is—to put it tactfully—mild; his association with Changing is primarily in the nature of a favor to Belle, whose friend he has been since her student days twentysomething years ago. The reason for his involvement is that Craft law—from the olden days around 1957, when there was only one Craft and it was Gardnerian—once mandated that all covens be organized in perfect pairs, just like Noah's Ark.

Magically speaking, it makes sense, but magical theory has never been popular with the masses. These days women outnumber men on the New Aquarian Frontier by about five to one, and the Noah's ark theory of Wicca has gone the way of the hula hoop and casual sex. Meanwhile, Belle and Daffydd go on like an old-time married couple, and Daffydd comes to coven about as often as most people go to church.

Introductions all round. Ned and Daffydd shook hands, then we arranged ourselves again and contemplated the menu. Daffydd ordered a Miller Draft. I had another Tsingtao. Daffydd and I did a little catching up—not much, as Ned wouldn't know any of the people and it wasn't polite to underline how much of an outsider he was.

Belle did bring up the subject of the picnic, though, which was Ned's cue to realize that I was not an outsider like himself, but one who had already attained Ned's desired goal. He shot me a look of betrayal.

"Not very big," Belle was saying. "I thought we'd start small. We can get High Bridge Park—"

"I know a lot of people you could get to come," Ned burst in, friendly and tactless as a Labrador puppy.

Belle looked at him, wanting to include him but taken a little aback. "We can put up flyers in the bookstores," she said, pitching it as if she were answering him. To me: "I'll call you next week."

"It sounds pretty exciting," Ned said heartily to the table at large. I winced, remembering a time when I would have greeted news of a gathering where I could meet actual Witches with the same maladroit glee.

"I hope you'll come," Belle said. "I'm sure Bast will post it down at the Snake."

"Is Bast your Witch name?" Ned asked me. I thought of telling him my parents were rogue Egyptologists and decided against it. "Yes," I said, and left it at that.

Eventually we got down to the fortune cookies and vanilla Häagen-Dazs with fresh ginger.

Ned waited—first with confidence, then with increasing apprehension—for the invitation that didn't come.

We settled the check.

Ned waited, waited, waited . . .

"I'll call you next week, all right, Ned?" Bellflower said.

"Sure." He smiled, covering his disappointment. "Or I'll call you."

He went to retrieve a jacket, and then went out the door.

Was it only my overheated and guilty imagination that told me how rigidly Ned Skelton schooled himself not to look back, not to linger, not to look in our direction?

"My place?" said Daffydd to Belle.

"Sure. Coming, Bast?" Belle asked me.

"Sure." I followed Daffydd and Belle out onto Broadway.

I hate this part. I hate having this much power over someone else's happiness, and I hate the possibility that because I'm tired, because I'm irritated, I'll use that power without thinking and leave welts on someone else's psyche that a lifetime can't erase.

This is why non-judgmentalism is so very popular. Because judging and choosing and making decisions means saying yes to one possibility and no to all the others. To do that is to take back all the responsibility that Society encourages you to give away.

Real freedom scares most people to death.

* * *

Daffydd has a little apartment on the top floor of one of those former stately homes that line Riverside all through the hundred-teens. His two rooms are decorated in English Docent Classic and contain more material than Belle's eight rooms and my one put together. Every possible wall is covered in bookshelves. Rolled maps, esoteric fan-tods, and books too big to be conventionally shelved jut from the shelves at all angles. You move through Daffydd's space at your peril.

We arrived. Belle took the hassock, I took the chair that went with it—both upholstered in villainous nappy mauve wool. Daffydd went into the kitchen and came back with three glasses and a bottle with a cork. He extracted the cork and poured, and sat down in a foldable wooden contraption that would have looked perfectly at home in Alexander the Great's RV. He looked at Belle. Belle looked solemn.

Apparently none of us had thought Edward Skelton was right for Changing.

Belle looked at me. I shrugged and pretended I was fascinated by my drink. It was a sweet dessert thing, the kind Belle likes. And me too, come to that. Wine snobbery is not among my virtues.

Neither, apparently, was acceptance. I sat there and disliked myself.

"I don't know if Ned Skelton would really be comfortable in a traditional Wiccan group," Daffydd said, when it became plain that nobody else was going to say anything.

To call Belle's coven "traditional" is just plain

inaccurate, but after a moment I thought I saw what Daffydd meant.

I looked up and saw that both of them were looking at me.

"Traditional meaning Goddess-oriented," I said. Daffydd smiled and raised his glass in salute.

"Hmm," Belle said, thinking it over. Lady Bellflower of the Wicca does not believe in magic, and doesn't trust hunches. "You think he might be uncomfortable with what we do in Changing," she said, trying it on for size.

At least half of the Craft traditions—and all the Gardnerian-descended ones—venerate the perfect balance of male and female energies, as symbolized by the God and Goddess. But to senses blunted by centuries of anthrocentrism, equal time often looks like preferential treatment—which is why, inaccurately, Wiccans are referred to as Goddess-worshipers, as if She had no consort.

I thought over what Daffydd had said. Ned Skelton didn't fit. He just didn't, for reasons I couldn't articulate. Saying he wouldn't like our rituals was as good a polite excuse as any for following a prompting that none of us could put into words.

"He's been working cyber-Welsh down at the Snake," my better self said, unasked.

Lorelli Lee is the Snake's general-purpose Pagan priestess. She works a different godform every Saturday; if Ned had been going any length of time he'd already been exposed to old-fashioned God/Goddess polarity as well as to rituals featuring Gaia Parthenogenete, Herne the Biker, Triple Hecate, and Gilgamesh/Enki.

Belle looked a little surprised. I could see her in-clining toward inviting Ned to an Open Circle with Changing so that everyone could meet him and I wished I'd kept my mouth shut.

"The picnic will give him a good chance to meet a lot of people," Daffydd said, coming to my rescue.

"Works for me," I said. Yeah. Maybe Xharina'd have an opening.

"That sounds good." Belle looked relieved, and that settled Edward Skelton's fate.

Not for Changing. For someone, but not for us.

Thinking about Xharina made me think about missing Books of Shadows. Belle already knew about Glitter's bereavement. A second loss—of which I wasn't even certain—could be only coinci-dence.

And Belle didn't believe in Witch Wars, didn't be-lieve in Pagan-on-Pagan lawlessness, didn't believe in the High Gothic silliness that so many of us love to indulge in, with secret passwords and coded recog-nition signals.

Secrecy is second only to conspiracy as a cheap euphoric decorator accent for Reality.

"Bast?" said Daffydd. I realized I was staring off into space.

"I was just thinking. About Mary, Queen of Scots," I added quickly, grabbing the first name that popped into my head so that Belle wouldn't think I was still wasting any brain cells on Ned.

"Why the sudden interest?" Daffydd asked, lean-ing forward.

"Well," I said, "Beaner's singing in that opera."

"And probably filled your head with all sorts of

nonsense," Daffydd said disapprovingly. Which meant he was, as Beaner would say, one of *Them*. "Interested in more unbiased information?"

Daffydd's day job is something in the soft sciences at Columbia, which means a lot of people send him free books. In a stunning conflation of resources and inclination, Daffydd's great passion in life is loaning books to people.

"Oh, sure," I said innocently. Hadn't Beaner said I should read more history?

Daffydd went off. He came back with a book. "Here," he said, handing it to me. "This should give you the basics."

Yeah. To start a fight with my closest friends and selected strangers over someone who'd been dead for four centuries. Oh, yeah—and eight years. I glanced at it. Academic press; small, heavy, acid-free paper. Blue buckram binding (the optimal meld of economics and respectability) with title-name-and-publisher stamped in gold (Optima 24-point for the title; Times Roman 18-point for the author's name; publisher in 12-point Caslon Antique plus stamp-blurred colophon) on the spine. It might even have come through Houston Graphics—we do a lot of academic press work.

"Call me if you have any questions," Daffydd said as I flipped through *Mary Tudor: A Rose in the Shadows* by Olivia Wexford Hunt. "History can be a little daunting when you're dropped into the middle of it, but it's just—history." Daffydd shrugged. I recollected that he's also a member of the Richard the Third Society; possibly Daffydd's interests lie in being spin doctor for dead royals in need.

The talk turned to the picnic and Belle's hopes for it.

Despite all of us being stuffed onto one island and/or five boroughs, the New York Metropagan Community is really fragmented. Some of us only meet at festivals far outside the city. Getting us together where we lived sounded like a better idea the more Belle pitched it—but then, Belle can talk almost anyone into almost anything.

We finished the wine. I agreed to coordinate Beltane Ecumenipicnic I. Daffydd insisted I take a cab home. He was probably more concerned about Mary than about me.

I live across Bowery (which used to be a high-rent district about 150 years ago) in the usual sort of crumbling Middle European prewar monocultural neighborhood that developers love to target. My landlord would love them to target it, too: my building's one of those *prix fixe* renter's dreams.

I had to pay three months' key money to get in, and my apartment strongly resembles a coffin—being ten feet wide and something more than twice that long with a fifteen-foot ceiling—but I've never regretted it, not with my rent being what it is.

I paid off the cab and went up five flights and opened three locks and I was home. I dumped my hat, jacket, and bag on my old-enough-to-be-an-antique-but-not kitchen table and went to check my answering machine. It used to be the only techno-toy I had, but at Yule I blew myself to a "portable" boom box with two cassette decks and a CD player. I doubt if I'll go any farther into consumer electronics, though—anything more would probably blow the building's wiring.

Even though it was well after midnight, I wasn't sleepy. I put on the water for tea, scaring the roaches half to death, and decided to take a look at Daffydd's book. The only other thing I had on my To Be Read pile was a romance by Pat Califia, anyway.

The water boiled. I made tea. I put Ned Skelton and peripatetic Books of Shadows out of my mind in favor of the musical question of what made someone four centuries dead hot news?

The basic facts Beaner had given me were correct. Mary Stuart, Queen of Scotland. Raised in the French court, the Manhattan of its day. Married at sixteen, widowed at seventeen. Superfluous to her de Medici mother-in-law (Mary wasn't in the succession for the French throne), she was packed off home to Scotland—away from glamour, away from sophistication, away from the meeting of like minds.

As far as I could tell, Mary did not handle being formerly important well. She was still a queen, but in Scotland she was a queen surrounded by people who were not at, who could not aspire to be at, the center of the world.

Every transplanted New Yorker—even those leaving voluntarily and for the best of reasons—knows the regret of leaving Avalon, Atlantis, the Hesperian garden that is the biggest and most golden apple of them all, and Mary Stuart was no exception. Her life was spent attempting to regain that same orient and enchanted sense of place that living at the center of the world had given her.

Looked at that way, Mary Stuart's life had a sort

of grisly relevance to modern times. If there's something you want, something you think you need to have to survive as the person you think you are, what price is too high to pay for it?

Compared to her cool Apollonian cousin to the south—Elizabeth the First, England's virgin queen of cities—Mary does not come off particularly well in the historical accounts. As Beaner said, a moron who failed Interpersonal Politics 101.

But as a woman who had been at the hub of her century's Manhattan glitterati circle and would do anything to regain that place, I understood her. She wanted the only important thing, and its gift was in the hands of others. Like Ned Skelton, she was desperate, obsessed—not to return to France, but to transcend France, by making her own island kingdom even more glorious.

Surrounded by incomprehension of what she was, maybe even knowing that what she wanted more than anything she could never have, but driven desperately to try for it . . .

That woman I knew.

Maybe too well for my peace of mind.

The sun was finally coming up when I turned out my lights.

# 3

I spent the next three weeks playing amanuensis to Belle's Beltane picnic, which grew from a New York–only event that maybe sixty people would attend to a happening welcoming every Pagan in New York, New Jersey, and parts of Connecticut.

Setting this up required more than just a phone call.

Belle got the permit to assemble from the Parks Department, and Dorje arranged the one-day liquor license so that we could legally bring kegs into High Bridge Park. The Cat posted our picnic on the appropriate computer bulletin boards, and I posted flyers in all the right places.

So much for the easy part.

What was slightly less easy was keeping any kind of track of *who* was coming, *what* (and how much) they were bringing for the potluck (and telling them over and over to *label* what they were bringing, to keep from accidentally poisoning someone with food allergies), and deciding who was in and who was out of the opening and closing rituals that Belle was working on.

Every time we got the cast list settled, something came up.

Either somebody couldn't invoke the East because Belle assigns the element of Water to the East on the fairly reasonable logic of there being an entire ocean in that direction, or they couldn't participate in a ritual where edged metal was used (even though we weren't using any).

Or they couldn't participate in a ritual where edged metal *wasn't* being used, since the one thing everybody found to pick on was the fact that Belle was being real nonnegotiable about letting people flash their *athames* in a public place. An *athame* is the purely ceremonial knife used by most Wiccans and Pagans in their religious rituals, and a knife is a knife is a real button-pusher, especially if John Q. Mundane sees sixty people in weird clothes waving them.

I wished it would only be sixty. *New York* magazine reports there are over ten thousand practicing Witches in Manhattan.

I hoped they weren't all coming.

But if they were, I bet they were all bringing potato salad.

In between bouts of damage control on the Ecumenipicnic came my stints at Houston Graphics. Ray'd liked the catalog, Mikey'd liked the catalog, even the customer'd liked the catalog, and it looked like a coffee-table book on the same theme was in the pipeline.

Despite which, it looked like being a bad summer for Houston—bad in the sense that the big jobs that kept the studio staff fully employed just didn't seem to be out there.

And that wasn't good.

Winter is Houston's traditional slack time, but every publisher going still does a Fall/Winter list. Fall/Winter pubdates mean that raw manuscript is turned into what you take to the printer from May through August—peak season for in-house art departments and places like Houston Graphics.

Not this year. And that meant lean times ahead.

There are other things I could do to pay the rent besides courting planned obsolescence. I could read tarot cards for money—good money in that, so I'm told, and working conditions no more uncertain than these. Only I have a small ethics problem with taking money for magic, and in my book, reading tarot is working magic.

I could go to work in an occult bookstore, but when all is said and done that's just retail sales, and even less job security than I had now. Not that I hadn't done it, but it was more in the nature of a hobby and I wanted to keep it that way.

I could hustle harder for freelance design work, I suppose, or pack up my portfolio and try to get a job at Chiat/Day or someplace like it. But the media in its wisdom has finally coined a term for us just-post-Woodstock folk (that's Woodstock *I*), and it's *slackers.* I'd hate to disappoint them.

Or maybe I'm just waiting for a sign to appear in the heavens.

And while I was waiting, it became April 30.

*    *    *

Beltane Eve is one of the Eight Great Sabbats in the Wheel of the Year and one of the two biggies, Samhain (Halloween to you) being the other. Changing would end tonight's Beltane ritual by turning out at dawn to watch a Morris side that was dancing its traditional greeting to the spring around 5:30 A.M. in Riverside Park. In addition to no sleep, that meant doing on Saturday everything that we possibly could about Sunday.

So we did.

Saturday at noon I opened the unlocked door to Belle's apartment. ·

"Don't do that!" Beaner shrieked.

The smell of baking bread hit me in a wave. I shut the door quickly before the draft could affect conditions in the kitchen.

"How can I—? Oh, it's you," Beaner said. He was wrapped in a white apron and looked like a demented alchemist.

"I love you too," I said, setting my overnight bag on the floor.

"We're having the last one for dinner. *This* one had better be perfect," Beaner said, meaning the bread. He went back into the kitchen. He'd be singing Leicester (*i.e.*, Robin Dudley) sometime this month, but what he was doing right now was baking a four-foot-long challah in the shape of the May Bride and Groom in Belle's kitchen (not to mention in Belle's oven, a harrowing achievement). I wished him luck.

I looked around. Ominous atonal wails came from the living room, where The Cat was checking out her portable sound system and tapes, including the background music for the rituals.

"Hi," I said, walking in. The Cat waved absently. The sun through Belle's curtainless windows haloed her Lady Clairol'd mop, a mass of interlocking dye jobs about the same color as the fur on Ilona's tabby cat—which is, of course, one of the reasons The Cat has the name she does.

"Sundance wants you. When he gets here," she said.

"Which is?"

"RSN," The Cat said. Real Soon Now. She went back to work.

Sundance arrived forty-five minutes later (traffic on the Long Island Expressway) and the two of us took Sundance's car to Queens to fill it with cased soda and kegged beer, his and my and Glitter's contribution to the picnic, as none of the three of us is any too domestic. Sundance is one of our few coveners with wheels—a consequence of having a job out on the Island—which is why a large portion of his contribution was cartage and haulage.

Glitter's book had never resurfaced. She'd recently purchased a new blank book, covered in lavender snakeskin, that she was filling in. I hadn't told her my suspicions that she was not alone in experiencing an unlicensed withdrawal from her private library. Glitter has enough problems in her life.

Sundance and I got back from the drinks run and I joined several other coveners up at the site of tomorrow's picnic, where we raked and cleared it (a process involving rubber gloves and tongs) and filled three large trash bags with other people's site garbage. I'd be guilt-free for weeks as a result of this burst of civic spirit.

Around the time it got too dark to work we went back down to Belle's to see who'd joined us in the interim. Everybody tries hard to make it for Beltane, and it was a weekend day to boot; we'd probably have a full house.

There was a large pot of vegetarian chili adding its scent to the baked bread when Dorje and Topper and Coral and I came in. Topper and Coral are married and will probably be the next to hive off from Changing; their presence today was a direct result of having been able to leave the kids with Coral's sister overnight.

"Who else?" I asked Belle. She was on the phone, but hung up as I came in.

"Ronin called—he'll be here after ten because he has to take Jeffrey back to his mother. Glitter's picking up some cookies and should be here in about an hour. Sallix had to cover for somebody in the emergency room today so she'll be here when she gets off shift."

"Actaeon?" Topper asked. They have motorcycles in common.

Belle shrugged. Actaeon usually shows up but never calls.

"Daffydd," she offered, as if he were the alternative entree.

"Hey, we'll all be here," said Coral. Being a mother, she can count.

"Lucky thirteen," I said. It felt good.

My coven—I think I'll keep them.

*   *   *

Five o'clock in the morning is *cold,* whether it's May 1 or not. We'd changed mostly back into inconspicuous street clothes to go out—although in Glitter's case that meant a purple lamé *hapi* coat—and, lightly garlanded, headed down to Riverside Park to watch something called the Seely Side.

Morris dancing is one of the Great English Mysteries, like cricket and warm beer. It dates back to the Middle Ages, and has been variously identified with Moors, or Moriscos (for Moorish dances), the Conversos, or recursant Jews, and the *sidhe,* the Fair Folk. There are eight men to a Morris "side" (although no one knows why it's called a side, unless it's a corruption of the Gaelic *ceilidhe,* or blessed).

This side was wearing white and green clothing, black hats with red and pink flowers, and came with a piper and drummer. Each dancer carried what looked like an ax handle without the ax and had belled garters tied just below the knee.

In addition to the thirteen members of Changing who'd come to watch, there were about a dozen other people gathered in the park, every one of us bundled up against the ice-cold breeze off the Hudson. Across the river, the rising sun gilded the topless towers of Fort Lee, New Jersey.

I think the dancers were a little surprised at the turnout—they weren't there to give a performance, after all; they were there simply because they were Morris dancers, and Morris dancers dance on May Day. While everyone agrees that Morris dancing is *some* sort of Pagano-folkloric manifestation, no one can agree on what sort, and your average Morris side is likely to be about as Pagan as, say, Fred Astaire.

So they danced as the sun came up. Clack of batons and ruffle of drum, skirl of the pipe over all, and the thump of the dancers' feet on the grass, a stubborn survival of ancient folkways in in the teeth of rationality.

At one of the breaks I went over to put a dollar in the piper's hat.

"Hey, um, Bast?" someone said behind me.

It was Ned Skelton.

He looked less like a fashion victim than he had at dinner, which might simply be the effect of the knee-length green wool cloak he was wearing today. He smiled hopefully.

"Hi, Ned."

He stopped to put money into the piper's hat—a ten; Ned must be feeling flush—and the two of us stepped back to give others the chance to be generous.

"So," Ned said. "How've you been?"

"Coming to the picnic today?" I said to change the subject. He was presuming an intimacy that didn't really exist between us, and it made me skittish.

"Yeah," he said, and looked suddenly sly. "I figure it'll be a good place to tell everyone the news."

My line was: "Gee, Ned, what news?", but I'd been up as close to all night as made no nevermind, and I wasn't in the mood to play more-occult-than-thou games with someone I was still having to try very hard not to dislike.

"Oh, good," I said.

"Wait till you hear," Ned said. "This is really going to change some people's minds about some things, *that's* for sure."

Terrific.

"I'm really looking forward to it," I said, in a tone

of voice that indicated that grouting the bathroom tile would be more fun. I saw it get through to him and I felt instantly guilty.

"Well . . . see you there," he mumbled, ambling off.

I might have gone after him. Apologized. Something. But just then the Morris dancers' piper and drummer started up again, making conversation impossible.

So I walked away. An hour later I'd forgotten all about it.

The morning fulfilled its promise and became what the local weathermongers call "one of the ten best days of the year" (of which, fortunately, there are far more than ten): bright, blue, and mild. Considering how many weather spells had been worked on its behalf I suppose it would hardly have dared to be anything else.

After breakfast, those of us who could stay for the picnic (as opposed to coming back for it later) started shifting things up the hill to the park; giving the area one last raking; hanging banners. Actaeon brought up his bike (as in Harley) so he could keep an eye on it, New York being particularly hard on those who wish to retain ownership of two-wheeled vehicles.

I noticed Belle's eye on me in the fashion that indicates that she wants a quiet word. As my conscience was currently clear, I drifted over to where she was.

Belle was dressed for the picnic in one of her Public Awareness Outreach ritual robes, the ones she wears when she's being an "official" Witch in the mundane world. It was tie-dyed in purple and pink and painted all over in gold pentacles, and made Belle look the way it was supposed to, which was harmless, accessible, and nonthreatening. The robe was cinched at the middle with a gold glitter sash and she was carrying a wand stuck through that: a carved rowan twig with a faceted crystal suncatcher set in the tip. She looked like the advance man for Glinda the Good.

" 'Scuze me, ma'am, can you tell me the way to the Witches' Picnic?" Belle ingenuoused.

"First star on the right and straight on till morning. Mind the teddy bears. They're having their picnic today too," I ingenuoused back.

I leaned against the tree. It was only eleven, and the official starting time for the Ecumenipicnic was one, but people were already starting to show up, heading for the folks wearing the green armbands that identified them as members of the host coven. I pulled mine out of my pocket and slipped it on.

"I saw you talking to Ned Skelton this morning," Belle said.

"Yeah. He's coming today."

With a "big surprise" for a cross-section of New York society that did not, on the whole, count charity among the virtues, I suddenly remembered. Maybe I could get to him first, talk him out of whatever public display he was planning.

"You know, Bast, you've been Third for quite awhile now," Belle began.

I tried not to goggle at her. I knew what was coming. I just hadn't expected it this soon, certainly not at the picnic, and most of all I couldn't imagine what Ned had to do with it.

You see, there are three levels of training in most

Wiccan systems, and when you've completed the third—or, as we call it, taken the third-degree initiation—you have the right to go forth, teach, and train others as you were taught.

Some people—Belle included—feel that this is an obligation, not a right. Unfortunately I've never been a great believer in doing things just because you can.

If I'm perfectly honest, the thought of that kind of responsibility scares me. It's not just that power corrupts. It's that power magnifies your every action, until nothing doesn't count. Nobody's behavior can be flawless under those circumstances. And I can't stand the idea of making mistakes with people's lives.

It's possible that some people might call me a perfectionist.

"And—?" I prompted.

"Well, you know that Daffydd and I didn't think that Ned was right for Changing, but *you* seemed to like him. You might consider training him as a working partner," Belle said delicately.

Witches, as previously mentioned, often come in pairs. And certainly if I hived off and began my own coven I'd need a teaching partner—and, in the traditional Gardnerian system, a male one. And it isn't that unusual to find someone you like and train them.

But *Ned?*

No, no, and no.

"I, um, actually was more concerned with being fair than—" I stopped, because the fact that my knee-jerk assessment of Ned Skelton was that he was a smug, self-obsessed little prick was not something I was proud of.

"Well, think about it," Belle said. "You know I don't want to push anyone into anything . . ."

"But you think I'm in a comfortable rut," I said.

Belle grinned. "Something like that. It doesn't have to be Ned. Think about it."

I made noncommittal noises. You don't tell your HPS and best friend she's being ridiculous, especially when you suspect she may be right.

But *Ned . . . ?*

There were somewhere between seventy-five and a zillion people in the park by one o'clock when Belle did the opening ritual. Since there was no way of counting them as they came in, there was no way to tell how many there actually were, but the park looked well populated.

Since this gathering was both ecumenical and a picnic, the ritual Belle had put together didn't bother with most of the formal Circle-casting ceremonial that a good half of us probably used at home. Instead it was more like a more elaborate form of the grace said at a Rotary luncheon.

Belle made the introductory invocation, thanking unspecified gods for their blessing of and attendance at our party, and we started around the Circle, invoking the Four Elements.

Tollah from Chanter's Revel did Water in the East, departing from Belle's "only a suggestion" script with a prayer to the whales cribbed from T. S. Eliot. In the North, a priest from the New York Odinist Temple called forth the blessings of Earth on the Children of Men, which also wasn't the way Belle'd written it and which drew a few PC scowls from the feminists among us.

Xharina was doing South.

She was a last-minute addition, since Reisha, who'd been supposed to do Fire, hadn't shown up by showtime. Since Belle's point was to show us how well we all worked together despite our varying convictions over which Elemental went in which Quarter and similar canonical conflicts, it would look bad if the opening ritual consisted solely of members of Changing. Hence the drafting of Xharina.

And since there was no chance for rehearsal, only the fact that everybody involved had lots of experience made it come off as well as it had.

So far.

Xharina stepped up to the plate. She was wearing what were probably—for Xharina—sensible shoes, with only a two-inch heel and a wide ankle strap. She also wore a black leather hobble skirt that had straps and buckles all the way down the back like a designer straitjacket. It was high-waisted, and above the waist she was wearing a black high-necked Gunne Sax blouse with big leg-of-mutton sleeves that covered her tattoos. She had on a cartwheel hat that must have measured three feet across, and she looked like a demented Gibson Girl.

But she rattled off her lines letter-perfect the way Belle'd written them and in a voice that rang the back rows without even trying. I wondered if she was something professional in the dramatic arts, as so many of us are. Not that it was any of my business. But maybe Beaner'd know.

A man named Nighthawk added a prayer for a successful space platform to his Air invocation in the West, and we were almost done.

Next, Beaner's *challah* made its procession to

where Belle and Lord Amyntor, High Priest of a Minoan trad coven somewhere downtown, were standing, and the gathered Ecumenipicnickers chanted to invest it with intention. And then we *were* done, and settled down to break bread.

While the loaf was passing, I wandered over to where Xharina was standing with what looked like two of her coveners (denim and leather), looking as if she wasn't certain that coming here had been a good idea.

"Hi. I'm Bast, from Changing. Thanks for helping us out."

"Sure. I'm a quick study; it wasn't that hard." She smiled; it made her look younger. "This isn't quite our usual scene."

"You mean chlorophyll, shrubbery, all that?"

She shrugged. "Yeah, I guess. Sunlight's awfully bright, isn't it?" she added with an exaggerated wince. "Um, maybe you can help; we brought stuff for the potluck but it's down in the van. I wasn't sure when we should bring it up."

*Or if you were going to stay,* I added mentally. There's nothing so conservative as the radical who has already rebelled, and as I've said, charity is not generally among the Community's virtues.

"Now's good," I said. The dismembered *challah* reached us and we each took a chunk, the two leatherboys looking to their mistress to make sure this was *comme il faut.* Neither of them was the one from the Snake, and I wondered what'd happened to him.

People were still getting here. The picnic was growing and spreading over most of the hilltop, and out of the corner of my eye I could see Sundance and Actaeon wrestling one of the kegs into place.

"If it's something heavy, I know an easier way up the hill," I said to Xharina.

The three of us—the guys answered to Cain and Lasher—went back down the hill to where a black van was waiting in front of a fire hydrant. The legend "Hoodoo Lunchbox" was airbrushed on the side, along with a phone number and a flaming guitar.

The man waiting with the van was costumed in Early Biker Slut: mirror shades, bandanna tied sweatband-style around the forehead, low-riding Levis, and no shirt under the open leather jacket. A Marlboro dangled from his lower lip. I was in love.

"Jesus, Xhar, I thought you'd gone out for a pizza," he said.

"Life is pain," Xharina answered, and all four of them laughed. "This is Arioch," she said, introducing him to me. "Arioch has a driver's license," she said, in the tone indicating it was another family joke.

"Printed it myself." Arioch grinned, and ground his cigarette into a brown smear on the sidewalk before popping the van's side door open.

Cain and Lasher horsed out two big Coleman ice chests and headed back up the route I'd shown them. Arioch slammed the door.

"Guess I'd better go park somewhere legal. See y'all next Christmas," he said.

"Pain is truth," Xharina said, and Arioch waved amiably.

The van rumbled to life, emitting a gust of blue smoke from its tailpipe, and wabbled off in search of parking. Xharina and I started back up the hill. On the way down she'd unbuckled her skirt so she could walk, and every step exposed her legs halfway up the thigh.

"So, um, I hear that Ned's going to join Changing," she said. We'd stopped to rest halfway up, but within sight of the revels. Someone had a tank full of helium and was assembling a lighter-than-air balloon garland.

"Well, he's pretty interested in finding a group," I said cautiously. Unfounded rumor travels fast, and I was very curious indeed to hear how the next sentence was going to go.

"He worked with us for a while last year," Xharina said, in the cautious tone with which nice people impart bad news. She made a face, hesitated on the edge of the plunge, and drew back. "I hope he works out for you."

She pushed herself to her feet, waved apologetically, and strode off to find her coveners and rebuckle her skirt.

What the hell?

So Ned had more experience than Belle'd thought, or at least more than she'd told me. As a factoid, it sat there in a nonrelevant lump. So he did. So what?

*Nothing to do with me, nothing to do with me, nothing to do with me,* I thought, chanting my mantra. I wished I'd remembered to mention Ned's surprise to Xharina. Maybe she'd know what it was.

When I got back up to the top of the hill the party was pretty well rolling. More people had arrived, food was being passed. Xharina was going to be popular—the ice chests contained two five-gallon drums of ice cream, kept rock hard in dry ice that smoked upon exposure to air like the proverbial witches' cauldron.

"Yo! *Bast!*" shouted a familiar voice.

Lace forged through the crowd, beer bottle in one hand, someone else's wrist in the other.

Lace is short for Lacey, which is Lace's honest-to-Goddess legal middle name. Lace works down at Chanter's Revel, which is the Wiccan, eco-feminist bookstore voted Most Likely To Be At The Opposite End Of The Pagano-Political Spectrum From The Snake—which makes it particularly odd that Lace, herself, is strictly a studs-and-leather dyke-type.

Of course, she *is* a vegetarian.

"Hey, girl, where you been keeping yourself? Isn't this a hoot?" Lace waved her Bud longneck at the immediate vicinity. "I got someone here I'd like you to meet."

The wrist in Lace's hand proved to be attached to a corporate-looking lass wearing a mint-green polo shirt and deeply impeccable khaki gabardine slacks. Her hair was cut in one of those expensive and severe earlobe-length designs. Her ears were pierced (once) and contained chaste gold knots. She was wearing pale pink lipstick and a smudge of taupe eyeshadow. In short, Gentle Reader, she was normal.

"This is Sandra," Lace said happily. "Sandra's a lawyer. Sandra, this is Bast."

Somewhere in the vicinity of this time last year Lace's lover had died, and it looked like Lace was ready to love again. I was glad of that, even if this particular relationship appeared to be doomed.

"I'm so pleased to meet you, Bast," Sandra said. She had one of those well-bred accentless dictions that was nearly a cliché. "Georgina has told me so much about you." She extricated her wrist from Lace's grip and held out her other hand.

Georgina is Lace's front name. Sandra and I shook hands.

"I hope it wasn't accurate," I said.

I valiantly resisted the temptation to ask her what her position was on Mary, Queen of Scots. Sandra looked polite but wary, as if at any moment I might do something horribly artistic.

"I hope you enjoy the picnic, Sandra," I said, with what would probably pass for sincerity. "Lace, it's good to see you again; I like the new color."

Lace's hair was bright cobalt blue. I saw Sandra dart a look of faint resignation at it. "But I'd better go see if Belle needs any help," I finished, before I said something stupid.

"See you," Lace said, happily oblivious. "C'mon, Sandy, let's go get something to eat."

I went off in the other direction, feeling as if I'd just avoided booking passage on the *Lusitania.* Why do people who already know it isn't going to work always find each other and try? I could not imagine Sandra and Lace even making it through the ninety-day trial period.

Of course, I might be wrong.

"Hey, Bast!" Glitter. She'd gone home this morning to change for the picnic, and the effect was blinding. "Seen Ilona yet?"

It took a moment to shift mental gears. Ilona. Lothlorien Books.

"She coming?" Odd. Not quite her scene, to quote the *patois* of my youth.

"She's supposed to be. I talked to her yesterday. She's bringing someone with her. Nephew."

"Who?" It was hard to imagine Ilona Saunders related to anyone.

"New partner in Lothlorien, she said," Glitter amplified. "Because she's buying the building. Don't know his name. She wants to introduce him 'round."

"I'll look for her—them," I said.

"Sure. Boy, did you see what Xharina was wearing? I'd never have the nerve." Glitter rolled her eyes and waved her glitter-lace batwing sleeves. Everything is relative.

I went off and collected a beer, a tofu burger, and a handful of oatmeal walnut chocolate chip cookies sprinkled with silver star-shaped jimmies certified edible. Nothing like a balanced diet, and this was certainly nothing like one.

And then I saw Ned coming up the hill.

He was wearing a black T-shirt blazoned with "The Goddess Is Alive, Magic Is Afoot!" in silver and carrying a white bakery box big enough to be holding a couple of pounds of cookies. I waved to attract his attention. He came over.

"Welcome to the Ecumenpicnic," I said. "I can show you where to put what you brought."

He looked hopeful and . . . not young exactly, but curiously unaged. As if he hadn't yet done much with his life, although he must be my age.

"Sure," Ned said. "Is everybody here?"

I felt ghostly warning bells go off at the question. One of the few points of etiquette nearly everyone in the Community observes is a healthful lack of curiosity about each other. People looking that hard for personal information are usually planning to use it, and not in any way you'd like, either.

"Well," I said cautiously, "we don't know exactly who's coming, and of course people show up and leave whenever."

Ned nodded sagely, as if I'd answered his question.

I herded him in the direction of one of the two picnic tables up here, which served as a sort of central depot for everybody's potluck offerings. Ned continued to explain as he walked.

"I want everybody to be here when I make my announcement," he continued with happy officiousness. He set his box on the table and opened it. Bakery cookies, as I'd suspected.

I felt a pang of alarm, and not at the cookies.

"Ned, could I have a word with you?" I said carefully.

He let me lead him off to an area that, if not uninhabited, was at least out of the main traffic pattern.

"Do you think you could tell me what you're planning to announce?" I asked.

Ned stared at me, his expression gradually changing from suspicion, to pleasure, to cunning.

"So you want an advance preview?" he said archly.

As opposed to the usual sort of preview?

"Well," I said, being driven, as Lord Peter Wimsey says in *Busman's Honeymoon,* to the inestimable vulgarity of reminding him who I was, "it *is* my coven putting the event on, so I'm one of the people responsible for making it run smoothly. So I sort of need to know." I gestured to the green armband.

"Oh." To my surprised relief, Ned seemed to think this was reasonable. "Well. You know the Book of Shadows?"

For one stomach-turning moment I though t he was confessing to stealing Glitter's, and then I realized he was speaking generally. I nodded, although it had to be a rhetorical question.

"Let me tell you a story," Ned said. He leaned toward me like he was trying to sell me cheap real estate. "No. Let me ask you a question. You're a Witch. You know that they're saying that guy made it all up; that Wicca isn't a real religion and all. What if I could *prove* that the Craft was hundreds of years old? No, *thousands.*"

I suppressed an impulsive rejoinder along the lines of having taken a religious vow never to buy any beachfront property in Florida, or bridges, or antique Books of Shadows guaranteed to have been passed down from ancient Atlantis.

"What if you could?" I said pacifically.

Ned frowned. I hadn't given him the answer he was expecting.

Oh, I won't say that it didn't matter passionately to any number of Witches, just that I wasn't one of them. If the sainted Gerald B. Gardner, founder of the feast, had been able to impeccably document his antecedents in his lifetime he might have done so or he might not, but the fact remains he didn't, nor has anyone who came after produced Wiccan documents that can be dated earlier than the late thirties, including that guy on the Left Coast who had the bad taste to publish the ones Gardner *did* leave.

And I was just cynical enough to think that any "proof" that surfaced after this long was proof that had been faked when there'd finally be money in it, New Age having become big business once everyone'd caught millennial fever.

"So you don't believe me?" Ned said, starting to look sulky.

"I thought it was a hypothetical question: What if you *could* prove it?" I said. Oh Goddess, don't let this be Ned's big announcement. I could choreograph the fights that would break out from here, and none of them would improve Ned Skelton's standard of living.

"Well, I *can* prove it. I've got an original Book of Shadows—a *real* one, an old one from before Gardner! I've got the real Book of Shadows—and I didn't have to be initiated to get it," he added smirking.

"Okay," I said. "So you've got a Book of Shadows." I wanted to tell him that I didn't care, but I doubted he wanted to hear it.

"You don't believe me!" Ned accused. "You don't think I've got it. But I do. It's called *The Book of Moons.*"

Ned watched me sideways, to see what impact this revelation had on me. The answer was none in particular, except that something called *The Book of Moons* sounded familiar.

Ned monologued on. Having gotten him started, I now realized, it would be almost impossible to shut him up.

"Now everyone will know all your nasty little secrets. I'm going to have it published. I wasn't going to. Books of Shadows aren't supposed to be published; you keep them secret so the rituals won't fall into unauthorized hands and lose their power. Everybody says Gardner made it all up, but I knew that wasn't true, because the Craft is thousands of years old, only there's no way to prove that it's real, because the rituals are supposed to stay secret. Except

now I have the proof. And it's where you and everyone else can't get their hands on it and suppress it,
and—"

I sighed.

"Ned," I said.

He stopped. He looked at me.

"Listen to me. I don't know you all that well, but
I've been in the Craft a lot longer than you have and
I don't wish you any harm. If you get up on a rock
here at this picnic today and make an announcement like that, people are not going to be impressed.
They're going to laugh at you. It doesn't matter
whether you're telling the truth or not."

Ned goggled at me like I'd just kicked his puppy.
"That isn't true," he finally managed to say. His ears
turned red, like the ears of laboratory mice.

"Yes it is," I said. "Talk to some people privately.
Talk to Lorelli Lee; you know her, the priestess at the
Snake? Nobody will believe you. And the way to con-
vince them isn't—"

"But it's true!" Ned interrupted indignantly. "It's
real. It's the spellbook that used to belong to Mary
Stuart—the queen. She was a Witch, see, and this is
her book."

That settled it. I was being haunted.

"You have the Book of Shadows of Mary, Queen of
Scots," I said, just to be sure I had it right.

Ned nodded. He rocked back on his heels. The
smirk had returned.

"And where did you get it?"

"I—bought it," Ned said, hesitating a little over
the obvious lie. I did my futile best to hold on to my
temper. Why does every newbie feel compelled to
reinvent the wheel?

When love and all the world were young (1963 or
so), there was a "tradition" of setting oneself up in
the Craft not through a process of training and initiation, but through theft of someone else's ritual
book. The person with the stolen book then covered
his tracks by inventing a provenance for his version
of the Craft that backdated it to somewhere around
ancient Atlantis, a pretty good example of one-up-
manship in a religion that can only reliably document its roots back to, say, 1947, if you really stretch
a point.

This form of spiritual cattle-rustling fell out of
fashion after about fifteen years, when everybody
suddenly decided it was much more chic to be creating a new religion than to be curator of a survival.
And at any rate, how you got your BoS stopped being
a big deal with the widespread dissemination of xero-
graphic technology and the computer disk. But here
was Ned, trotting out that old chestnut about somehow acquiring a legitimate antique Book of Shadows
just as if no one had ever heard it before.

"You must think we're all pretty damn stupid
around here," I said to Ned in my most courteous
tones. "The only cliché older than that is saying that
your grandmother initiated you into a secret family
tradition. Nobody is going to believe you, Ned. I
promise."

He stared at me, slowly going red. Probably nobody he'd ever spoken to had been so blunt. We in
the Community tend to avoid confrontation, as a
rule. We don't argue. We just go away.

"If you want to be a Witch, okay, you're a Witch,"
I went on. "Now all you—"

"You can't threaten me!" Ned blustered. "You

don't know what you're talking about—and you're wrong, too!" He stalked off, ears flaming.

I sighed. I hadn't handled that particularly well, but maybe I'd at least bullied him into shutting up. I didn't particularly give a damn—and besides, he'd thank me for it someday, providing he stayed in the Community.

And if he didn't, he'd be even less my problem than he was now.

Or so I thought at the time. As it turned out, I was wrong straight across the board.

# 4

I walked—or stalked—back through the picnick-
ers, heading for the beer. I wondered what Beaner
would do if I told him that Mary Stuart was Queen of
the Witches. Or Daffydd, who could at least tell me
whether she'd been mixed up with sorcery according
to Official History.

Her cousin Elizabeth had been. Lizzie's court sor-
cerer was that learned Rosicrucian Doctor John Dee,
who worked with that highly suspect Irishman, Ned
Kelley. Most historians agree that Dee, no matter
what else you may say of him, was devout and sin-
cere—and managed to survive the experience of
casting a horoscope for both a reigning queen and
the princess in waiting.

Ned Kelley (not the Aussie Bushranger of similar
name popularized by Mick Jagger, trust me) is another story entirely. Profane, irreverent, and Irish, he
was constantly implicated in shady deals and criminal acts, escaping prosecution due to his Court con-
nections. Kelley's claim to fame and Dee's patronage
is that he is alleged to have been a medium: he saw,

so he said, angels in a "shew stone," or speculum, that he had given Dee directions on how to build. Evidence suggests Kelley was not entirely fraudulent, at least not all the time: Dee's creation of the glorious and abstruse system of Enochian Invocation from the stuff of Kelley's visions is the jewel in the crown of Elizabethan sorcery.

I doubted that Ned Kelley (who vanishes from history as mysteriously as he appears) had ever felt left out and awkward and socially maladroit.

Or had been on the outside wanting in. Or back in. Like Ned Skelton. Like Mary. Who, according to our Ned, was a Witch, with a genuine Book of Shadows that had somehow managed to escape the notice of her inquisitors and jailers at the Fotheringay Resort for Inconvenient Queens.

Damn Ned, anyway; the woman was dead four hundred years and change and I couldn't escape the spookily persistent feeling that she was someone I'd spoken to this morning—that she was someone I could still advise. *I know how you feel. I know how you hurt. But there's no cure; there's never any cure once they've shut the door. You can't trust other people for your happiness, Mary—people are just too damn fickle.*

But no. And if not Mary, how much more so not Ned? Their problem was exactly the same: If there's something you think you need to have to survive as the person you think you are, what price is too high to pay for it?

Is any price too high?

I tried to put all webby ethical brain-twisters out of my mind, and succeeded reasonably well with all the distraction on offer. I even talked myself into a reasonably good mood, or at least a better one. What with one thing and another I knew most of the people here; I wandered through, collecting greetings and invitations and information about this, that, and the other gathering. Reaffirming old friendships, laying groundwork for new ones.

And I heard tales. Tales that slowly, oh so slowly, started to frighten me.

Otterleaf was a Gardnerian High Priestess who ran a training coven in Astoria. She was trying to figure out how to get in touch with her Queen, who'd moved to Arizona, because she couldn't find her Black Book and needed to get a new copy.

Crystal had braided her hair with knots of ribbon and had painted both cheeks with rainbows for the picnic, but despite the Sparkle Plenty affectations she was a pragmatic Faery Trad of the Victor Anderson stripe (Victor being another of the Grand Old Men of the Craft) who ran Starholt Coven and the Cyberfae BBS. She was sure her book must be around *somewhere,* although she hadn't seen it for the last month.

Lord Amyntor, the Minoan HP from downtown who'd opened the picnic with Belle (he had "friend of the family" status because Beaner'd dated him for a while last year) was talking about the *new* book he was putting together to replace his old one.

Now that I knew what I was listening for, the undercurrent was everywhere: not outright admission, but an uneasy sort of "here comes the hangman" humor. Having your book stolen had become a black joke that everyone understood.

As in: "And then there was this funny-mentalist who was so dumb he burned a *blank* Book of Shadows."

Glitter's wasn't an isolated incident. It was the leading edge of a plague.

But no one was fingering anybody for thief. We— the Community at large—had no suspects. None. And that was odd in a bunch famous both for getting its exercise jumping to conclusions and for having an Official Summer Feud each year to wile away the time till Hallows.

I looked around. I saw people with bubble pipes, people with balloons, people with flutes and guitars and celtic harps (live music later), and people carrying hula hoops and ferrets. There were people wearing chain mail and wearing chiffon and waring full Klingon battle dress and wearing baseball caps with stuffed antlers attached.

Party clothes. Persona clothes, for people who had found a safe space in which to wear their inner child on the outside for a while. I wondered if the person with the ever-growing BoS collection was here. I wondered if all the BoS's had been stolen by the same person. I wondered if all the ones that were missing had been stolen. I wondered if I was losing my grip on probability.

Who would steal Books of Shadows? Who, and why—and, dammit, *how?* These people were New Yorkers; their doors had *good* locks.

Belle waved to me, from a kaffeklatsch of other New York–area covenleaders. Ah, Bast, play your cards right and this time next year you too can be among them.

Although after our last conversation, Ned probably wouldn't join a coven of mine if I asked him. Not that I was going to.

Where had Ned gotten the "Mary, Queen of Scots" Book of Shadows? Stolen? Or self-created out of the mass of public material? And why choose Mary for his fall guy? She wasn't exactly the most plausible candidate.

Echo answereth not.

I wandered, cataloguing the people I knew who weren't here. No Cindy, no Julian—none of the downtown Ceremonial Magic crowd who thought of Pagans as Bridge and Tunnel People. No Santeros, or representatives of any of the other tropic-zone religions: Huna, Voudoun, Candomblé, Brujeria. Only the one Odinist.

No Ilona, with or without partner. I wondered if she'd changed her mind about coming. I couldn't see Ned at the moment, which was a blessing. I had what Ned wanted, and there was no way on earth for me to give it to him, no matter whether I wanted to or not.

Was Ned Ilona's new partner? Now *there* was a daunting thought. Fortunately I didn't shop there much.

I hove in sight of the beer. Beaner was standing next to the keg with someone I hadn't seen in too long.

"Niceness!" she trilled, in a voice only bats and dogs could hear. "Niceness is all!" She and Beaner broke into an impromptu duet à la Eddy and McDonald of "Ah, Sweet Mystery of Life."

"Hi, Maidjene," I said. She turned around and mimed a heart attack brought on by ecstasy.

Maidjene is a coloratura soprano. She has brown hair, brown eyes, and is the sort of person of whom people say, "Oh, what a pretty *face* she has." Maid-jene is the founder of the Niceness Wicca tradition, in which she parodies Craft politics—a routine that has a small but appreciative audience. She'd come to today's picnic in her alternate Pagan *persona,* the Niceness Fairy, and every exposed body surface was covered in multicolored glitter and sequins.

She was wearing a size-60 fuchsia polyester nightgown and marabou peignoir over her T-shirt and overalls and carried a Lucite wand topped with an enormous glitter-encrusted star. More fairy dust flaked off every time she waved it.

I refilled my beer and she got a Coke and we found a place to sit and play "How long has it been", Maid-jene interrupting herself every once in a while to bless passersby with "Concentrated Essence of Nice." In between these minidramas, she confessed that she and her husband were, as she put it, "giving up."

Larry, Maidjene's oh-so-mundane husband, had been a staple of Community folklore for years. Maid-jene had gotten religion after they'd married, and Larry had not been pleased.

"And now, one day I come in and the basket's gone through my things and helped himself to a big chunk of my notes."

, "Well, damn," I said. I wondered if Maidjene was out on bail. "What happened?"

"Well, he denied it and I told him he could deny his ass out the door and into a hotel." She pronounced it midsouthern fashion: *ho*tel; Maidjene and Larry are both originally from someplace in Tornado Alley. Kentucky, I think. "May the Nice be with you!"

"And then?" I asked, fascinated. Even if it was some floating Book of Shadows bandit and not Larry responsible for the theft, his eviction couldn't happen to a nicer newt. He'd made a pass at me, the one HallowFest he'd come to, on the expressed theory that Witches believed in casual sex.

"Lawyers are talking, he's in the hotel down to Route 17, and I had to go back to my Queen for my real book. But *fortunately* the whole Nice liturgy was published in *Enchanté* last year, so I've got that. And by the way, you hear Lark might be coming back East this fall maybe even in time for HallowFest? Selene says he said—Nice Makes Right!—that last quake did for him and he's not staying anywhere that the four seasons are Drought, Riot, Fire, and Quake—Niceness Rules!"

HallowFest is the big Pagan festival held in upstate New York every October—four days of fun and frolic in the mud and freezing rain. I go every year.

"We'll have to have a welcome home party for him," I said. I'd known Lark pretty close to very well a few years back. I wondered if he was coming back unattached.

"And let me say this about that," Maidjene went on, in her trademark nonstop rattle, "if you're looking for a working partner—Niceness Upon You!—you'd be one helluva lot better off with Lark even if he's commitment shy—which we *don't* know for sure, and he may have changed—than with Fast Eddie Skelton if you ask me and even if you don't." Even Maidjene had to stop after that one and pause for breath.

"You know him?" I said, surprised. Maidjene lives

in the occult wilds of northern New Jersey. A long way for Ned to travel.

"Whooo-eee!" Maidjene shook her head, shedding sequins. "Had him in an Open Circle. *Once.* I tell you, you want somebody joggling your elbow, you call in Fast Eddie—Have a *Nice* Day! He not only knows what you're doing, he's got a better way to do it—Niceness Rules! Wah!"

"It sounds to me like he's been around," I said.

"You want to know how far, you ask Reisha. Or Lorelli Lee. Everybody knows him. Nobody likes him. He's pushy," the Niceness Fairy said, wrinkling her nose.

Belle must have known all this. There was no way she could not. Okay, so she did, and didn't tell me in the name of impartiality.

But while it was true that people could not-click for reasons having nothing to do with whether or not they were good people, if Ned had as much experience in the Community as Maidjene said and was still acting as jerkishly as he had today, the odds were against his being one of the innocent ones.

Maidjene saw someone else she wanted to talk to, and I gravitated to the edge of the party, where you could look down the hill and see the real world. Reality, as the saying goes, is a nice place to visit, but I wouldn't want to live there. Not what passes in this modern day for Reality, anyway.

I watched the escape of a fugitive ballroom, my mind full of things I hadn't yet mashed down to thinkable-size portions. Behind me, The Cat's sound system slid lower in volume and then cut out, and in the sudden silence I could hear musicians tuning up: flute, guitars, and harp.

"Hey, everybody—*hey!*"

I winced. Ned. And, from the sound of things, not 100 percent sober.

I turned around and walked back into the picnic. There was a clearing-within-the-clearing that provided seating by way of two stumps and a big rock. The Cat's tape deck was there. So were two bemused Crafters with guitars, a man wearing satyr horns and carrying a silver flute and a tin pennywhistle, and a woman in medieval clothes with a harp.

And Ned. Just as if he were following a script I'd handed him titled "How to Make of Yourself a Permanent Stupid Joke and Outsider in the New York Pagan Community." He was standing on the rock, plastic cup of beer in hand, face flushed, obviously ready to make his announcement.

I felt the stunned horror that you feel watching an accident slowly happening right in front of you. You don't want to believe in it, but it's right there, and there's nothing you can do to stop it. I wasn't even angry at Ned at the moment. You aren't angry at the car that's stalled in the path of the oncoming train.

"Ned!" I yelled. Maybe I could stop him.

He swung around toward me. He sneered.

"*She* doesn't want me to tell you!" he shouted, which got him even more attention and me a lot of stares.

"She doesn't want me to tell you because she wants to suppress it! But I don't believe in secrecy!" Ned ranted on. A few people cheered. I saw The Cat crossing left behind him, heading for the tape deck. Probably on orders from Belle.

"I have a genuine Witch's Book of Shadows—a real one. It's hundreds of years old and has all the true authentic *old* spells and rituals, and I—"

Someone laughed. The flutist played a derisive skirl. And whatever Ned had to say next was drowned out by jeers, catcalls, and people producing various bombastic takes on the rest of his speech. Ned looked stunned. He'd finally seen the train.

I'd told him. We've heard it all before. And though many of us would desperately love to trace our religion in identifiable form back across thirty centuries, it's still a joke. There've been too many disappointments.

For a moment more, Ned tried to shout over his audience. Then he just stared—angry, humiliated, betrayed. I thought he might be going to cry.

The Cat flipped a switch, and "Corn Rigs and Barley Rigs" (she'd sampled it off a tape off *The Wicker Man*) filled the space. Nearly everyone there knew the song, and some of them started singing. The harpist began improvising against it.

Ned jumped down off the rock and ran. A couple of people tried to stop him, but he jerked past them. I was on the opposite side of the crowd from him; even if I thought I could do any good, there wasn't any way to get to him.

The Cat said something to one of the guitarists, who nodded and began fitting himself into the music. The Cat took her sound levels down, and after a ragged few beats the tune was being carried live by two guitars, a pennywhistle, and a harp. Someone started to sing a set of words—not Bobby Burns's originals, but our own invention. The people within earshot quieted down to hear them.

I hurt for Ned Skelton, legend in the making. He could manage to live this down if he could pretend he'd been making a joke.

But he hadn't been, and I knew it. I think nearly everyone there knew it.

He'd been serious. And he'd brought his seriousness to people who he thought would understand. And we'd laughed at him. And he'd never understand why, not in any way that would help him heal, though it's really very simple.

When it hurts too much, you laugh.

There was nothing I could do for Ned, and the picnic seemed to be under control. I wanted to get the preceding scene out of my mind and looked around for something that would help me do it.

That's when I saw him. The stranger.

He was standing at the edge of the clearing. He was wearing a sportcoat and an open shirt with his neatly pressed khakis and oxblood loafers, and the reason he looked out of place wasn't really his clothes, although they were part of it.

Although it's not quite PC to say so, it's also unfortunately true that the men who belong in the Community actively dis-belong elsewhere. They've made a choice, conscious or otherwise, to drift from the normative centerline of Western culture, and the first place that drift appears, as the poet says, is as a sweet disorder in the dress. Even Daffydd exhibits this subtle sartorial mark of Cain. Studded leather or slogan T-shirts, there's a concrete fashion subtext there for the discerning eye.

This spectator radiated none of these cues. His haircut was a thing of expensive beauty, of the sort rarely seen above Seventy-second Street. And, confronted with the spectacle of a woodland clearing full of Us, he was not in the least discomfited.

No one else had much noticed him yet. I headed toward him, bracing myself for everything from an evangel interested in the state of my soul to a reporter to an innocent bystander looking for a lost dog.

"Hi," he said when I approached. "Is this the Witches Picnic?" The accent was English, pure BBC Received.

He was around my age, with light brown hair and eyes the color of expensive Scotch.

"Yes," I said cautiously.

"Is it okay if I stay?" he asked. "It isn't a private party, is it? Oh, I'm Stuart Hepburn." He held out his hand.

His Englishness shouldn't have made any difference, but it did. I shifted mental gears and shook the hand. It was innocent of rings. He wore a very well-bred and expensive watch on a black leather strap.

"Hello, Stuart," I said. "My name is Bast. What can we do for you?"

"Well, I saw the poster for the event and thought I'd take a dekko. I'm interested in learning more about . . . Wicca?"

He pronounced the name as if he weren't quite sure he was pronouncing it right, but he hadn't boggled at mine. I smiled. He smiled.

"Sure," I said. "There're a lot of people here who can answer your questions. Would you like a beer?"

We sauntered back toward the food. I was steering Stuart in Daffydd's direction because Daffydd is
erudite and respectable and makes the Craft seem
like nothing more than an enthusiastic exercise in
reconstructive anthropology. But when I got close
enough to hear what he was saying, I was sorry I
had.

"Look. If Henry hadn't forsaken the Catholic
Church, none of this would have happened," Daffydd said. "Mary was the logical heir, the rightful
heir—"

Oh god. Not her again.

"Yes, and if she *had* got her hands on England
we'd all be speaking Spanish today," Beaner shot
back with passionate inaccuracy.

"*¿Y eso te molesta?*" Ronin said, and those who
could follow the Spanish laughed.

"The point is—" Beaner said.

"The point is, even though the Great Divorce was
driven far more by the need for the dissolution of the
monasteries and the reappropriation of capital by
the Crown—" Daffydd said.

Stuart put a hand on my arm.

"Before we go any farther, there's something you
ought to know," he said, nodding toward Daffydd
and Beaner.

My heart sank. *Uh-oh,* I thought. *Here it comes.*

"I'm the rightful king of Scotland," Stuart said
gravely.

I stared at him. The corner of his mouth quirked
upward in mockery. "Hepburn," he explained. "The
Earls of Bothwell. If you go back far enough."

Thanks to my recent reading I was ready for

him, although I was beginning to sympathize with Beaner's desire to scream when That Woman was mentioned.

"James Hepburn, Earl of Bothwell, Mary's third husband," I said. And related to the Bothwell that'd tried to assassinate James the First by magic, leading to the Berwick Witch Trials, one of the most famous cases in the history of the subject.

"Or as we prefer to think of her, Bothwell's second wife," Stuart said solemnly. He smiled again, encouragingly. I breathed an inward sigh of relief and decided conditionally to like him.

He was crazy, all right. But he seemed to be crazy like us.

"Are you married?" Stuart asked me a few minutes later. It took me a moment to recognize the question for what it was: mundane world small talk.

"I used to be, but I got out of the habit," I volleyed back glibly. It's true, actually.

Just within hearing the historical debate raged on, with Belle hovering nervously around the edges. Sandra had joined it, as a voluble partisan of Elizabeth the First, Christendom's most puissant prince (her words). I sympathized with Lace's bewildered expression. I have enough trouble staying afloat in one century at a time.

"And what's your interest in the Craft?" I said to Stuart, steering him away from the new English Civil War.

"Well, I admit that I'm coming to it from an historical perspective," he answered. "I understand that the witchcult can trace its roots fairly far back."

"Oh, more or less," I said. It's true enough.

There's material in the BoS that appears nearly word for word in a manuscript dating from the early 1300s, which is no proof of antiquity for either the book as a whole or our religion.

"I don't suppose you'd like to tell me all about it?" Stuart said. I glanced at him. He flashed me a charming smile. I wished I'd worn more upscale clothes.

"Mmmn," I said, not committing myself to anything. Sheer force of habit. "Your best bet is to do some reading. Talk to people. There're a lot of books on the subject; you could do worse than hit up some of the occult bookstores and look at what's in print."

I gave him some titles and some addresses, and the talk turned general. He was over here visiting. He was in business for himself and could set his own schedule. He was interested in Wicca and was looking for someone he could talk to about it.

He hinted that it wouldn't be all that unpleasant to see me again. I made it as clear as I could manage that I didn't think it would be any hardship without quite coming out and saying so. Explicit declarations would have to wait until I had a better idea of his agenda.

Like rock stars, doctors, and movie producers, Witches have to resign themselves to the fact that there will be people who don't love them for themselves alone, but for what they can get out of them, from social introductions to magical initiations to free spells cast on their loved ones. I wasn't quite sure how to peg Stuart yet, and keeping my distance until I found out who he knew and who knew him couldn't hurt.

Eventually we went amiably in our separate directions, me wondering if Stuart was what I needed to take my mind off Julian and Stuart thinking whatever Stuart was thinking. I honestly thought I'd never see him again.

This was not my day for being right.

The Closing Ritual went off smoothly at around six o'clock, when most Ecumenipicnickers (we'd drawn over two hundred people, Belle thought, and I thought she was being conservative) were still here but thinking about leaving. Xharina had collected her troops and her ice chests and left about four, saying she hoped to see me again at HallowFest. I hoped she'd heard enough about missing books to make her give her covener another chance, but I doubted if I'd ever know.

The closing ritual was essentially the opening ritual in reverse, where we thanked the Powers that Were for attending and seeing to it that nobody was beaten up, struck by lightning, or afflicted with food poisoning.

The speaking parts were cast entirely from Changing, both so that other people woudln't feel obliged to stick around and to give Changing—which was, after all, responsible for all this—the chance to shine, now that all the politicking had been done. Once the ritual was over there wouldn't be much else in the way of site aftercare, Pagans making a you-should-pardon-the-expression religion of leaving their campsites cleaner than they found them. At least when someone else was looking.

Topper and Coral were Priest and Priestess, standing in the center with their kids Jamie and Heather, who would someday be able to boast, like many of their generation, that they were hereditary Witches, raised in the faith of their foremothers—and finally, after all the lies and unprovable assever-ations, it would be true. If their parents weren't arrested first.

Ah, political correctness, the gentle art of mind-ing somebody else's business.

It had been a long day, but fortunately I could do this particular set of closings practically in my sleep, even if I couldn't enunciate as clearly as Xharina. I kissed my hand to the Lion in the South and passed the metaphysical ball to West, North, East again, and home.

And the First Annual Beltane Ecumenipicnic was over.

Of course, Belle was already talking about *next* year.

# 5

**M**ost people get particularly stupid just after pulling off something large. It's the letdown of having worked real hard and now it's over and you're left chock-full of energy and intention with nothing to apply them to.

The moral is, don't do anything when you're tired, when you're rattled, when you're pumped full of adrenaline.

It's just too bad that nobody ever takes their own good advice.

What I did take advantage of was that seniority which hath its privileges to show up around eleven at Houston Graphics, which meant that Ray was waving a phone at me before I quite got the door open.

Most of us didn't start life intending to end up at Houston Graphics, and Ray is no particular exception. He used to be a dancer—Jazz Ballet of Harlem and a bunch of Broadway shows—until something happened. When Ray wears shorts to work you can see the scars the surgery left; big black *S*-shaped marks on the inside and the outside of his knee.

So Ray took up graphic design. Mikey Pontifex owns the business, but Ray runs it. And keeps us all happy. More or less.

"No, she just walked in," Ray explained to the phone. "Yo, Kitty—it's for you."

Ray Lawrence also has a differently abled sense of humor.

"Hello?" I said cautiously into the phone. Unless America has declared war on Manhattan, *nobody* calls me at work between nine and five.

"Bast?" Glitter. Her breathing was jerky, as if she'd been running.

"Yes?" I waited for the punch line.

"Ilona's dead. Someone killed her."

No, not running. Crying.

I looked at Ray, who was waiting, with the full force of his personality, for his phone back. I wished Mikey would put in a second line.

"Where are you?" I said. "Let me call you back."

Glitter was at work. I gave Ray back his phone.

"I'll be right back," I said, heading for the door.

"Nice of you to stop by," Ray said. Such a wit.

I hoofed it downstairs to the deli next door, which has in addition to other amenities, a phone. I ordered a *caffe latte* and called Glitter back. By that time she was crying so hard I had difficulty in making out what she was saying.

Ilona was dead. Sometime Saturday. The land-lord had found the body. There'd been a break-in and she'd died.

"How did you find out?"

"Maura told me." Maura is a cop who frequently arrests the people who later become Glitter's clients. "She knew I knew her, and she— And they— It isn't *fair!*" Glitter wailed.

*Life is pain,* I remembered Xharina saying to Arioch. Yeah. And pain hurts.

I stayed on with Glitter for several quarters' worth of phone time while my coffee grew cold and undrinkable. There was nothing to do, nothing for anyone to do but the police and the coroner. Ilona's death was just another point on the curve plotting the urban evolution toward the apocalypse.

I got back upstairs forty minutes later. The phone rang as I came in. Ray picked it up. "Houston Graphics."

There was a pause.

"It's for you," Ray said to me.

Thank the good Goddess that Mikey wasn't there. I took the phone from Ray.

"Yes?"

"Is this, um, Bast?" The caller sounded like an anemic bassoon.

"Yes?" Who the hell was it? No one's voice I recognized.

"I got your number out of the phone book. Remember, you said where you worked? I hope it's okay to call you," the voice went on forlornly.

No, it wasn't. Ray was staring at me with a fixed non-expression.

"Is there something I can do for you?" I said to the phone in carefully correct accents.

"This is Ned Skelton," the forlorn voice said. Now

I recognized it—and I remembered that I had indeed mentioned Houston Graphics' name, somewhere during that dinner two weeks ago.

"Ilona's dead," Ned told me. "I came to work this morning, there was a police notice on the door, and I went down to the station like it said and—"

I'd completely forgotten that Ned worked for Ilona. There was no way I could cut him off without being cruel. I semaphored apologies at Ray. He turned back to the job he was working on with ostentatious disinterest.

"I have to see you," Ned said desperately. "Please!"

I started to tell him okay, but he must have heard it as a refusal. Maybe Ned Skelton was used to hearing a lot of refusals.

"No!" he said. "You don't understand. It's not for me. I've heard a lot about you. I'm sorry, I'm sorry, I never meant— At the party. You were right. At the picnic. It was wrong. It's a sacred trust, you can't just— Everybody says you're fair. You have to— I need you to— It's just a *box*. That's all it is, I *swear* it. Just a box, just for a few days. Oh, please, *please*—"

Despite the ease with which we bandy the word about, most people have never heard someone actually beg. Ned was begging now, and I found myself willing to promise almost anything to make him stop.

"Yes. Okay, Ned. I'll do it. It's all right," I soothed.

I wasn't quite sure what I'd agreed to. Something about a box for a few days. At this point I didn't really care.

"I'll do it," I repeated. Ray gave me a funny look.

There was a brief silence. Over the open line I could hear the faint sounds of Ned trying to be quiet.

"Can I bring it over now?" he said at last. My jaws ached in sympathy with the effort he was making to hold on to his self-control.

"Yes," I said. I asked him where he was. He told me: uptown, on the West Side. I gave him directions. He said it would be about an hour and a half. I told him we could go have lunch.

I handed the phone back to Ray.

"Finished with your social life?" Ray said.

"And the horse you rode in on," I told him sweetly. "His boss was murdered Saturday night."

"Bummer," Ray said, accepting my apology. He was specing a job, and I looked over his shoulder to see what it was. Ned and his box would be here about one-thirty, but meanwhile I was out of work.

"You can have this when it comes back," Ray said, laying the typesheet down on the copy and making obscure notes in the margin. Designers make good money—Ray was one of the few Houston Graphics inmates making a living wage.

"Great," I said. But not that great because it would be at least two weeks and maybe three before StereoType got the raw type back to us, and what was I going to do in the meantime?

"So you got anything for me now?" I said.

"You think you deserve work, after tying up the phone all morning?" Ray asked.

I didn't dignify that with a reply.

"Couple'a binding dies," he said, relenting.

I went over to the shelves where incoming and

outgoing jobs are stacked and found the jobs. The type had already been set; it was paper-clipped to each mock-up.

Even though book cover design has long since been supplanted by book jacket design, book spines—like the one on *Mary: A Rose Among the Shadows*—are still stamped with title and author and publisher's logo. The way the stamp looks is up to places like Houston.

There were six of them; ten hours' work if I dogged it unspeakably. I took them back to my board and got to work.

One of the better fringe benefits of this business is that jobs are frequently no-brainers. While I filled my pen and cut and ruled my board and kerned (adjusted the spacing between the letters by hand) the waxed repro into place I had plenty of time to think about things I didn't want to think about.

Ned. Ilona. Mary, Queen of Scots. Stuart Hepburn. Urban violence. Passion and free-range stupidity. And what would happen to Lothlorien now? Would Ilona's partner take it over?

If it wasn't unfair, you wouldn't know it was Life.

Fortunately Royce got into work before Ned did, which put a little glamour into my day. It was 12:40 by the clock on the wall, and it was instantly obvious what had taken Royce so long.

This was a Dress Day.

Royce was wearing a little brown frock with white polka dots, a saucy brown straw cocktail hat with a scrap of a veil, full maquillage, and white gloves. The shoes were modern—brown ankle-strap Capezios—but everything else was vintage.

Royce collects. It's a good thing he's skinny, or he'd never find retro clothing to fit him.

He saluted Ray and waved to me and went over to his desk. Nobody said anything—Tyrell'd used to, but he'd stopped.

Beaner camps, on the reasonable presumption that performing artists are obliged to provide street theater, but Royce has never queened it in my presence. He's always the same person no matter what he's wearing; it's just that sometimes he's wearing dresses: a warrior in the cause of *laissez-faire*. I smiled to myself and went back to work.

Ned arrived more or less on schedule. I'd finished one die and started a second. I wasn't in a lot of hurry. When I'm not working, I'm not earning.

He was carrying a stuffed knapsack (what male New Yorkers carry because purses are for sissies). I went over to the door when I saw him.

"Come on in," I said.

He stared in all directions when I let him into the studio. It's just one big room, not quite square, with a rectangle-shaped bite out of our space near the door to make room for restrooms for this floor of the building. In the corner thus created stands the stat camera, blue and hulking and requiring disassembly for cleaning by Royce every Tuesday morning. We're supposed to kick back a dollar a stat to the studio if we use the machine for our own projects, but nobody ever does.

The rest of the room contains Mikey's desk, Ray's light table, innumerable metal bookshelves filled with past successes, and a bunch of four-foot-high free-standing partitions sheltering light tables and stools, set at right angles down the middle to give everyone a little storage area and the illusion of a private work space.

"This your place?" Ned said.

I looked him over carefully. Ned Skelton had the particularly brittle, sharp-edged look of someone who'd had a severe shock and was currently refusing to admit it. A confrontation with mortality, even if it's only someone else's, tends to have that effect. There were dark soot-bruise smudges under his eyes and his skin looked over-scrubbed. He was wearing jeans and a work shirt and was doing a complex impersonation of someone who was just fine.

"I work here," I admitted.

"They know you're—you know?" he asked, lowering his voice conspiratorially.

An odd question, on the face of it.

"They wouldn't care if they did know," I said, which is true. Both Mikey and Ray are remarkably uninterested in anything that doesn't make them money.

"What would happen if somebody told them?" Ned persisted.

I gave him a sharp look, wondering if agreeing to help him had been a mistake.

"Nothing would happen, Ned," I said with a sigh, "because nobody cares. Now, where's this package?"

He dragged it out of the knapsack, which deflated conspicuously. The package was a brown cardboard box, about thirteen by twenty, and eight inches deep. The box had probably originally been used to ship books in and was almost completely cocooned in monofilament-reinforced strapping tape, as if Ned were afraid something inside might get out.

He held it out to me in a fashion suggesting it was a large box of chocolates I should be pleased to receive. Ray, Seiko, Eloi, and Royce watched with interest.

I took it. It was heavy—two or three pounds—and solid. I wondered what was in it. I was afraid I knew.

But *how?* That was always the question: *How?*

"Just for a few days, okay?" Ned said.

"Sure," I said. I shook it gently. Nothing shifted.

"Be careful," Ned said warily. "Don't open it."

"Let's go get lunch." I stuffed the package into the storage shelf in my carrel next to *The Casablanca Cookbook.*

Around the corner from the deli there's a restaurant that ought to be more upscale than it is considering how convenient it is to New York University and CBGB's. It has a fine selection of imported beers, and the only decent thing on the menu is the burgers.

I ordered a burger. I warned Ned. He ordered cheesecake and a Coke.

"So what are you going to do now?" I asked. Now that your former employer's been murdered, I meant. I didn't wonder why Ilona was dead. This is New York. There's hardly ever a "why."

Ned shrugged. "I'm okay. I've got another job. It was only part-time. Lothlorien."

I'd thought we were going to talk about Sunday and other things, like the possibility the box Ned had handed me contained the fictional *Book of Moons* that he'd been raving about at the picnic. We were not, it developed, going to talk. Ned's discovery of Ilona's death seemed to have shoved Sunday's picnic so far into history for him that bringing it up would be as relevant as discussing the siege of Troy.

But I couldn't leave it alone.

"About Sunday, Ned—"

"They're all wrong. And they're going to be sorry. It really *is* old," he said. "And it's real Wicca. Margaret Murray was right."

He said it as if it were the only thing he had left to hold on to. It might be.

Dr. Margaret Murray was a nice, respectable Egyptologist until the day she got the notion that the medieval witch-trial records should be taken literally. She wrote three books of progressively less mainstream scholarship: *The Witch-Cult in Western Europe, The God of the Witches,* and *The Divine King in England,* in which she links more of the English nobility to Wicca than any writer until Katharine Kurtz—and swears that Wicca is a religion stretching in unbroken practice back to the caves at Lascaux.

"Why are they going to be sorry, Ned?" I asked in my best imitation of Belle's psychiatrist voice.

Ned's eyes slid away from mine and he flushed. "They just will," he mumbled. "You're— Look, you're not *mad* at me, are you?" he blurted out.

It was not a question one adult should ask another. It contains too much acknowledgment of subservicence, of emotional comfort that depends on someone else's whim. But Ned Skelton was—still— looking for someone else to provide that. Looking for someone else to give him what he thought he needed: power.

As the ad campaign for the *Godfather* movies reminds us, power cannot be given, only taken. The

great flaw in the Western mind-set is the conviction
that power must always be taken from someone else.

We all have power. It can't be given to us. And
when we take it, we take it *for* ourselves, not *from*
anyone. This is the great mystery.

The secret is that there is no secret.

"No, Ned. I'm not mad at you."

Not yet, anyway. But I could get that way.

"What's in the box?" I added.

And why leave it with me?

He winced as if I'd slapped him and gazed plead-
ingly at me with those hangdog hazel eyes. "Could
I . . . Could I tell you next week?" he asked. Humbly.
"I will. I promise. I'll tell you next week, if you'll just
keep it for me now. Please?"

I coudln't stand it.

"Sure," I said gently. "It's all right." I'd make a
lousy dominatrix.

I hunted around and found one of my cards that
has my business name—High Tor Graphics, Freelance Design Work—and my legal name—Karen
Hightower—and nothing else on it. I wrote the studio
number down. "It's better to call me after five,
though."

Lunch straggled painfully to its end. I paid my
check. Ned paid his. We went to the door.

"You won't open it, will you?" Ned asked. "You
promise?"

The chill I felt then was entirely the product of my
own overactive imagination. While I suspected that if
I opened Ned's box I'd be unhappily surprised, I
couldn't pin my conscious mind down to the form
the surprise would take.

"Why did you want *me* to hold it?" I asked, unable to resist any longer.

"Everyone says you—" Ned hesitated and actually shuffled his feet. I was filled with agonizing curiosity about "everybody."

"They say you'll keep your word."

*A Witch's word is law.* Belle had told me that during my training. It doesn't mean what it sounds as if it does. What it means is that oathbreakers make lousy magicians, and what you say, you'd better do.

"I won't open it until I see you again," I promised. "Call me soon, okay?"

"Sure," Ned said.

Later I'd say to myself that some part of him already knew what was going to happen, but hindsight's always twenty-twenty.

I was back in the studio by three. Seiko'd left, which left me, Chantal, Royce, and Eloi—and Ray, of course. I applied myself to the binding dies, and by the time it was five o'clock I'd finished three of them.

I decided to save the rest for tomorrow. Maybe there'd be more work then, depending on the calls Mikey'd made today.

I left Ned's package on the shelf. It was just as safe there as it'd be at home, and this way I didn't have to lug it around.

I grabbed my hat and headed out.

When unsettling things happen, people seek solace in normalcy. I headed for the Snake.

When I got there, Elvis was blessedly silent and the store was reasonably empty. I had the section marked "Witchcraft and Women's Mysteries" completely to myself. It had been restocked recently.

*The Grimoire of Lady Sheba* by Lady Sheba. *The Complete Book of Witchcraft* by Raymond Buckland. *A Book of Pagan Rituals*, Herman Slater, ed. *Mastering Witchcraft* by Paul Huson. *A Witch's Bible* by Janet and Stewart Farrar. The book alleging to be Gerald Gardner's unpublished notebooks, which almost certainly wasn't.

And that was just the top rack.

In short, more published, legally accessible books of Wiccan and Pagan rituals than any one person could possibly need.

So who was stealing the homegrown ones? And why? And—and this was what was driving me crazy—*how?*

If I could only figure out "how" I'd be willing to suspect Ned of it, since my gothic imagination couldn't think of any better contents for the box he'd left with me. I freely admitted this, in the privacy of my own brain.

Unfortunately for my future as a lurid fiction writer, I couldn't make all the pieces fit.

"Why" would be simple: revenge.

But after that, things started falling apart, starting with "How" and ending with "And Then What."

Skip, for the moment, how Ned, my villain-elect, got into all those apartments without leaving a trace, and where did that leave you?

Nowhere. Because someone who knew the Community well enough to know where to go to steal all those books woudln't have pulled a dumb stunt like that hoaxical announcement at the picnic.

Or would they?

And, that aside, even if I was willing to jump to the conclusion that there was a stolen BoS—or half a dozen of them—in the box Ned had left with me (though unfounded suspicion was no grounds for breaking a promise), I couldn't come up with a reason for his leaving them with me.

Why me?

Nothing made sense. Whichever way I tried the frame, it fell apart.

"Hey, Bast," someone said from over my shoulder. A voice I recognized.

It was Lorelli Lee.

Lorelli Lee is one of those people who reassures me that looking straight is still an option here on the New Aquarian Frontier. She is of average height and weight and build. She has mouse-blond hair that she wears in one of those shoulder-length styles that would be invisible in any office in the country, a not unreasonable number of holes punched in each ear, and vision-correcting glasses that do not suggest that she is the visiting shootist from any one of a number of left-wing military organizations.

She wears skirts. She has been known to wear them with coordinating jackets. She maintains a lucrative and responsible accounting practice, standing between a number of fringy small-business owners and freelance service providers (such as Yours Truly) and the unveiled wrath of the IRS.

"Ilona Saunders died, did you know?" I said. "Over the weekend."

"No!" Lorelli's protest was the automatic one of someone who didn't know the other person particularly well.

"Saturday night," I said. Which explained her absence from the picnic, now that I thought about it. "And—"

"Hi, Bast," Julian said, appearing not quite in a puff of smoke. "I was hoping you'd come in. Per Aurum's just sent us their spring shipment, but I haven't gotten around to getting it out."

He looked, as usual, like a dissolute priest. It is rumored that he attended seminary somewhere and left before taking his vows, but I try to ignore rumors.

"You want to tag them and check off the manifest for me? Off the books," he added.

With the way things were going at work I could use a second job, but I didn't want to put my non-relationship with Julian on such a mercantile basis.

"Store credit—wholesale," I counteroffered, and Julian actually smiled.

"Deal," he said, and held out his hand. We shook on it.

It was the first time I'd ever touched Julian.

And that was how I wound up sitting in the Snake's secret temple at six o'clock at night with seventy-five hundred dollars' worth of wholesale jewelry plus manifest.

I always derive an immense furtive kick every time I go back here, although the Snake's "clandestine" temple is probably the best known secret in the entire Community. The rack that holds the robes (back right, next to the figurine candles) swings out to reveal the hallway that leads to the bathroom at one end (important urban survival information) and the temple at the other. I'd sorted through the boxes waiting in the hallway until I found the one from Per

Aurum, collected the box and everything else I needed, and gone back into the temple to work.

The Snake's temple (and lecture hall) is actually the back third or so of the shop footage. The walls are painted matte black, and someone—probably Tris—has installed enough track lighting to qualify the place as a theater of the absurd.

At the moment two floods—one blue, one purple—were focused on the built-to-spec altar that was still set up from the O.T.O.'s weekly Wednesday ritual. I sat down on the bottom step of the altar and ripped the box open, being careful not to cut into any paperwork that might be on top, assuming Per Aurum'd remembered to send it.

I found the invoice. Good. I looked it over. No surprises.

Notwithstanding that their name translates from the Latin as "By (means of) Gold," most of what I unpacked in the Per Aurum shipment was silver.

Item: Thirty-six plain pentacles, the interwoven star in a circle that no self-respecting Neopagan would be without; a dozen each of small, medium, and large. The mainstay of the Snake's business, even in these troubled times.

Item: Two dozen medium pentacles set with assorted stones: lapis, amethyst, hematite.

I counted them and stacked them in neat piles, each one in its slippery self-seal bag, and checked them off on the invoice. After I had everything logged in, I could price them for sale, a simple matter of multiplying the wholesale cost by 300 percent—a process called triple keystoning.

I said the Snake's merchandise was overpriced.

I continued my explorations. A dozen pentacle rings, sterling. A dozen moon and star rings, ditto.

Six Art Nouveau Moon-Goddess or maybe Fairy Queen stickpins. Or maybe they were angels; angels were a hot property just now, for people who liked the idea of a twenty-four-hour feathered yenta in their lives.

Pentacle earrings, pairs. A dozen—no, the manifest said a dozen and a half. I hunted through slippery plastic packets to find the other six pair.

"How're you doing?" Lorelli asked, coming through the secret door. She was carrying a pizza box and a couple of containers of coffee. I looked down at what I held in my hand and tried to decide whether this was a Celtic pendant or a Norse pendant.

"Norse or Celtic?" I replied, holding it up. She studied it for a minute.

"Norse. They're gold with pewter accents. The Celtic ones are pewter with gold accents."

Lorelli sat down on the step next to me, careful not to dislodge the small piles of jewelry, and set down the box. "They're both regular," she said of the coffees, which in New York means cream, no sugar. I took one.

"Thanks," I said.

"Dinnertime, anyway," Lorelli said. "I made Julian buy."

I took a slice of pizza.

"You said Ilona'd died?" Lorelli said, taking up the conversation where it'd been left.

The talk drifted around Lothlorien's demise,

Ilona's death, and mutual acquaintance. I filled Lorelli in on the details of the picnic.

"And it's funny," I added, not really thinking about what I was saying, "but everyone seems to be missing Books of Shadows."

Lorelli choked, and sprayed a mouthful of coffee halfway across the room.

"Really?" she said, when she could speak. "Because mine's gone, too."

"I keep wondering if I just misplaced it," Lorelli said, in the tone of one trying an unworkable theory on for size anyway. "It was in my office with the account books. It looks pretty much like them. But then it was gone."

I began removing silver pentacles from their bags. I wrote control numbers and grossly inflated prices on tiny white tags and started threading them through the bail at the top of each one.

"When?" I asked, seeing what a direct question would get me.

"I'd wanted to use something in it for last Saturday. So, a week ago Thursday I missed it."

That would be around the twenty-eighth of April, about two weeks after Glitter lost hers. I bet if I could get real answers out of people, I'd find that practically everyone's book had vanished sometime in April.

Why?

Lorelli took a pen and a sheet of sticky dots and began pricing the Celtic pendants.

"Somebody broke in?" I suggested.

"I keep the room locked, there's a gate on the window, the front door is locked." Lorelli recited the list in a singsong monotone, as if it were something she'd gone over and over. Probably she had. "I don't have a group meet at my house, I'm not all that out, cyber-Welsh is a self-created trad." She stopped, shrugging. "I can replace just about all of it," she added.

"Sure," I said. I finished tagging the small pentacles.

Her head was down, bent over the sheet of labels. Colored lights turned her skin and hair a ghastly, ghastly color.

Translated from the Paganspeak, Lorelli did not have either a study group or a coven meeting at her house, she was not "in your face" about her religion to the outside world, and since cyber-Welsh was a self-created Neopagan tradition, that meant she'd assembled it herself from public—and published—material, so she didn't *have* any hidden unpublished secrets to steal.

Locked, she'd said, doors and windows both. If either'd been forced, she would have said. So it was another "walks-through-walls" reasonless theft.

If it was a theft at all—but Lorelli seemed both reliable and organized.

"You know, I must just have misplaced it, you know?" Lorelli said wistfully.

I knew.

I finished marking up the shipment and went and told Julian he owed me sixteen dollars of store credit. On the way out I ran into Stuart Hepburn.

"Well, hello there," Stuart said. He smiled. I smiled. He still looked well favored and aggressively normal.

"I see you're taking my advice," I said.

"This is quite a place," Stuart said, looking around.

To call the Snake "quite a place" is like calling Versailles a little villa in the country. I admired Stuart's English reticence.

"I work here sometimes," I said. "Can I show you around?"

I showed him the Witchcraft section and made some recommendations. Stuart poked through some of the Books of Shadows but didn't seem to find what he was looking for.

"But none of these is really old," he said.

"The really old stuff is in the case behind the counter," I told him, "But you won't find any Books of Shadows there. Just grimoires."

The talk turned personal. Stuart asked if he could see me. I forbore to mention that he was looking right at me, since that wasn't what he meant.

I wondered, perversely, if Julian could see us back here and if he was jealous.

Not a chance.

I said yes. I gave Stuart the card with my home number on it. He said he'd call tomorrow or Wednesday, since he had some business appointments that weren't too definite yet. He left.

I wondered if I could successfully get through a date without making too big a fool of myself, which at least made a nice change from everything else I'd been wondering about lately.

I got home around nine, unlocked and relocked my door, got myself a beer and a shot, and realized with regret that it was again approaching the time of year during which even a large fan in my only window would not render my apartment inhabitable. I picked up *Mary Tudor: A Rose in the Shadows* and popped a cassette containing, among other light classics, "Tom O'Bedlam" into my newest electronic toy. When I hit "play" it was the middle of the song.

*"With a host of furious fancies / Whereof I am commander—"*

Beaner'd said it was a political ballad about Mary, Queen of Scots. The lyrics were printed on the lyric sheet folded into the cassette box, and made about as much sense three hundred years after the fact as the jokes on "Laugh-In" do after a slightly shorter period. Gibberish.

*"The punk I scorn and the cutpurse sworn / And the roaring boys' bravado—"*

The past is a foreign country; they do things differently there.

Thus the beginning of another perfect week in the Attitude Capital of the World.

# 6

Tuesday was normal until a quarter after five.

I was at Houston that late because High Tor Graphics, my freelance business, had picked up some work: a complete series of invoices and tracking forms for a company calling itself "Sopht-Wear."

The Cat could have run them up in an hour on a CAD-CAM system.

I glared at the pile of technology in the corner of the studio. Last year Mikey'd bought a low-end CAD-CAM system for the studio, intending to obsolete all of us (the hand-drawing of charts and graphs is a good third of the studio workload). Fortunately for job security he had not internalized the knowledge that the hardware would have fits when the temperature spiked over eighty degrees.

Since my place of employment, Houston Graphics, maintains its fingerhold on solvency by not squandering money on useless inessentials like air-conditioning (or heat in the winter), the temperature in the studio is well over eighty much of the year between June and September.

Eventually Mikey'd decided the system he'd bought was simply unreliable, and none of us had any intention of enlightening him. I think a commercial air-conditioner would blow every fuse in the building anyway.

The phone rang.

"Bookie-Joint-Can-I-Help-You?" I rattled off on one lungful, because Mikey only owns the place until five. Since he doesn't want the studio phone answered after five, we answer it that way. Most of life's problems can be worked out with a little creativity.

"This is Ned," Ned said. I shot a not-quite-willed glance down at Ned's package. "I need help."

Ten minutes later I hung up the phone. I'd promised to be there as soon as I could.

Ned had indeed been a Skelton of his word. Though his apartment had been burgled Monday night, he had waited to call me about it until after five P.M. Tuesday.

Nothing was taken. I'd asked. And Ned had spent today doing the right things, so far as filing reports and buying new locks went. What he'd wanted had been a subtler form of help.

Ned wanted his apartment blessed, so that the energy the burglar had brought—call it the stamp of his personality, for lack of a more precise term—could be removed. A psychic cleansing, to go with the physical tidying up.

There was no doubt that I'd go, although he didn't know it. The last time someone'd asked me for help, I'd been too late.

I went home and packed my Danish bookbag with what Belle calls my Traveling Priestess Kit: *athame,* charged water, incense, sea salt, and a few other things. Then I hit the subway. Ned had given me directions. They weren't too hard to follow, but the destination they led to was a bit of a surprise.

Fast Eddie Skelton, part-time bookstore clerk, lived on West End Avenue on the lower Upper West Side (above Lincoln Center, below Columbia), at an address where apartments rented for more than I made in an average month. I found Ned's building without much trouble.

There was an ambulance and a cop car in front of it, flashing red and amber keep-aways at a small huddle of licensed gawkers.

I saw them from across the street: the cops, the wagon, the crowd. It was unseasonably hot, but I felt cold down to my fingernails.

*Coincidence. It's coincidence, it's coincidence, it's—*

I stayed where I was, as if to move would be to participate in this hideously routine street theater. It was someone else. Of course it was. How could it be Ned? He was young, healthy, and I'd spoken to him on the phone no more than an hour ago.

The two EMTs with the gurney came out of Ned's building. It had a dark plastic mummy-bag on it, zipped-up shut the way there is when there's a dead body inside. They loaded it into the ambulance, and slammed the doors, and got inside, and drove away.

A few minutes later the cop came out and got into his cop car and did the same. Just another of our forty daily homicides here in Baghdad on the Hudson.

I was certain of what I'd find when I went into the building. Certain the way you are in nightmares, outside of logic. That ought to mean I didn't need to go, to see for myself, but a few minutes later, when the crowd had diffused, I went in anyway, telling myself I was wrong.

I had the spooky hopeless feeling you have in tragedies, knowing you're going to say your lines and it isn't going to change the outcome. Insisting, meanwhile, that everything was fine, that Ned and I were going to go out for drinks.

The lobby was a study in genteelly-diminished elegance: gilded egg-and-dart molding, elaborate ceiling fixtures, a fireplace that might even have worked once. Ned's apartment was first-floor front.

There was a notice on the door, and bright yellow tape. Not a surprise. Never a surprise—didn't you know that Witches can see the future? I gulped and gulped, swallowing hard, even though I knew what the notice said because I'd seen one before, at the last place I'd gotten too too late.

I tried the door and banged on it anyway, reaching through the tape that told me this was a crime scene, this was a murder.

"Hey, lady! Cut it out!"

I jumped. Guiltily.

The speaker was the tenant of the apartment across the lobby. He teetered on the verge of looking like a Brooklyn truck driver, glaring at me. He was probably an expensive lawyer.

"If you're looking for the super, he's gone. The police took him out in a bag." He seemed to derive an immense personal satisfaction from being able to say that.

"Super?" I said blankly.

The man frowned, thought about slamming his

door, and decided not to. "Someone shot him, lady," he said. Then he did shut the door, but quietly.

I turned around and looked. There is a futile and useless push-bell beside most New York apartment doors. This one had a little white sign over it that said "Super—1A." Ned's apartment. Ned's other job.

I thought about knocking again and didn't have the stomach for it. Besides, there was no one in there to hear, was there? Someone had shot him.

*Shot him dead. Ned is dead. First he said and now he's dead. Ned is dead, dead is Ned. Did someone shoot him through the head?*

I felt faint, and cold, and unwilling to face facts. I didn't want to think about this. Ned had called for help and I'd come too late. Again.

I didn't want to unleash the yammering guilt-monster that said this was all my fault, and I didn't want to face the fact that I ought to call the police and tell them that I'd spoken to Ned and when.

Would Ned still be alive if I'd taken a taxi instead of the subway?

Would I be dead?

I wanted to go home.

But I didn't go home. I went back to the studio. I even took a taxi.

I was terribly unhappy, as if I'd missed the only chance I would ever have to meet someone that I could have loved if we had only met. But I didn't and hadn't and wouldn't have loved Ned Skelton. Who, between 5:15 and 6:35, had been permanently cut from this eon's performance of the Traveling Reality Roadshow.

I wished I'd taken a taxi to his apartment.

All the way back to the studio the wheels kept

repeating the same sentence: *Ned is dead, Ned is dead, Ned is dead . . .*

I'd been too late again.

I got back to the studio around seven-thirty; it was just starting to get dark. The building was still open. If you're there after eleven you're there for the night; the super puts the outside shutters down then.

I was shaking so hard I dropped the keys three times before I could let myself into the studio. There was nobody here, just me and the rats and the roaches. I flipped on all the lights, even going around and turning on the tensor lamp at each workstation. I wanted light, lots of light.

*Ned is dead.*

Something didn't make sense. It wasn't just the reasonless guilt. *Something didn't make sense.* That was why I was afraid. Irrationality is the greatest terror of all.

But I didn't know what it was that didn't make sense. It was something lurking down among the unexamined assumptions in the dark unconscious, and I was here, on the surface of my daylight mind.

Ned was dead.

The box. Was it why he had been murdered?

*"I won't open it until I see you again,"* I'd promised. Well, now I had.

I went to my carrel and picked up the package he'd left with me. Still heavy, still thoroughly sealed. I grabbed a mat knife, knowing I was probably going to slice myself with it. I did; the tape was tougher than I expected and the knife got away. The razor point slid a narrow red line down my left wrist—

lengthwise, the way the ancient Romans used to like to open their veins. It didn't bleed much.

I finally got the package open.

"Fuck. Fuck you, Ned Skelton. Fuck you, you son of a bitch," I said hoarsely.

It was Glitter's book.

It was Glitter's book and more. Two and three and four and five and a sheaf of printout in a data binder that had Lorelli Lee's name and address on it (six) and a slim handmade book of red leather embossed with a bull's head (seven) and another one swathed in bubble wrap that I could see had a binding chipping and cracked with age (eight).

I counted. Eight.

I got up. I walked around the studio. I made a list of the phone calls I was going to make and decided not to make them. I made a new pot of coffee. If the phone had rung I think my heart would have stopped right then, but it didn't.

And then the coffee was ready and I poured it and stared into my cup and prayed to the Goddess very hard, notifying Her that I was willing to trade any amount of three A.M. craziness and anxiety attacks for the next two years for the ability to think clearly now.

And after a while my mind stopped sprinting around my brain like a nervous gerbil and I was able to pull the timeless disinterest around myself that good magic comes from.

You can say that the Goddess answered my prayers or that She gave me the strength to answer them myself; it doesn't matter. What did matter was that I was ready to make some preliminary decisions on what I would do with the contents of that box.

I went back to Ned's box of stolen secrets.

What are the Gods worth on the open market? What price a hotline to gnosis, or a designer-direct package of Revealed Truth? Can a person *need* religion, and, granting that, did the intensity of Edward Skelton's self-perceived need legitimize his theft?

No. Ned's thefts were neither legitimate nor excused. I understood the desperation that could lead to what we must politely term temporary moral confusion, but it still wasn't right, or even necessary. It was just a fact that I had to work with, because Ned was beyond being able to do so.

Who was stealing Books of Shadows? Ned Skelton.

I'd always had "why." And now I had "how," didn't I? Because working at Lothlorien had been Ned's part-time second job. And now I knew what his first job was.

Ned was a building superintendent. A nice white English-speaking strong young man to service the upscale needs of upscale tenants on the Upper West Side. And because the upscale tenants had upscale toys they also had upscale locks. State-of-the-locksmith's-art, and Ned had very nice master keys to fit them. He could come and go anywhere, invisible in a work shirt and pants and jangling bunch of keys.

And now he'd never do it again.

Now it was my problem.

I liked to think that he'd realized that stealing Books of Shadows wouldn't take him where he wanted to be, that he'd been working himself up to returning them. It didn't make the position he'd put me in any easier, though. I was the one who was going to have to return them, dodging awkward questions of how I'd gotten them. If I could.

I went through the books again more carefully.

Here was Glitter's, unmistakable. I could find her and give it back. No problem, except maybe with the explanation. And Lorelli's, ditto—in fact, I had her home address; I could mail it to her anonymously and explain later.

The red book belonged to Lord Amyntor (how not, with all those bull's heads?). I didn't know his real name, but Belle might. Beaner certainly did, and where to find him, too.

That left five. One was Gardnerian, Otterleaf's. One was Xharina's. One was Crystal of Starholt's— she had a heavy hand with rubber stamps involving fairies. One book belonged, apparently, to "Diana–27," someone I'd never heard of, even at the picnic.

I was able to put names to all these books so easily because one of the things a Witch puts into a Book of Shadows is her own Craft name: the name she takes when she decides to become a Witch. The name she's known by in Circle. The first page of my BoS, for example, says "The Book of Shadows of Lady Bast of Changing Coven." It wasn't much as a real-world address went, but it did mean that with a little asking around I could get these back to their rightful owners.

And none of them, my mind informed me with irritating inclusiveness, could possibly be the Mary, Queen of Scots, grimoire that Ned had been puffing off at the Ecumenipicnic.

But the box wasn't empty yet. I reached in for the

last item, the one so carefully wrapped, when none of the others were.

One old book, about twelve inches square. I eased it out of the bubble wrap. The cover was dark brown leather, cracked and showing tan where the glazed surface had flaked away. The spine was hubbed and channeled; old-style bookmaking from when books were sewn, not glued.

I picked it up. It was lighter than it looked. I opened it carefully.

The pages were real vellum, which is to say lamb-skin scraped until it's thin and soft and white as paper. Age had turned the pages tea-colored, their edges toast-colored and chipping.

I steadied it with one hand and opened the book carefully to the first page.

*Marie,* it said. And *Le Livre des Lunes.*

The Library of the Moon? No, my French was bet-ter than that. The *Book* of Moons.

Not a Gardnerian book. Nor Alexandrian, or any other this-century Wiccan tradition. It didn't even have the "family resemblance" that my book did to Lord Amyntor's.

I turned a few pages. They were covered with an-tique writing, head to foot and gutter to margin. The script was long and looping, pale and brown with age, insanely regular even though the pages weren't ruled. The words and sentences ran together until the page blurred into an even, unreadable pattern. The noodle script was broken by a string of symbols that looked vaguely like a Celestial script called "Crossing the River," familiar to me from hours spent with Francis Barrett and other nineteenth-century mages.

Despite my best efforts, the edges of the pages crumbled at my touch. I turned carefully to the last page. The writing stopped abruptly a few lines in. The rest of the page was filled with a signature, faded to brown after all these years but written large in defiance:

*Marie the Queen, by the grace of God Queen of England, Scotland, and Ireland.*

I closed the book and set it back in the box.

*The Book of Moons.*

My life had suddenly turned into cheap pulp fiction. This called for another cup of coffee at the very least. I got it and drank it and retreated to the far end of the studio.

I drank my coffee. I wished I still smoked.

*The Book of Moons* of "Marie la Reine"—Mary, Queen of Scots. Maybe real, or maybe just a forgery, but *old;* you could smell it rotting away every time you opened it; a more intense, concentrated version of the pervasive odor at Lothlorien Books.

Which did not exist anymore, because Ilona had been murdered during a burglary.

And Ned, who had worked there, had also been burgled—a fitting karmic commentary on his covert agenda—and murdered—which was not.

No, wait. That wasn't quite right. Ned had been burgled—at least, he'd told me he had—Monday night. But he was murdered *Tuesday* night.

Why the twenty-four-hour delay?

I gave up on self-restraint. I went over to Eloi's carrel and picked up the pack of Camels I'd remembered seeing there, making a note to buy him a full pack in penance for looting. I lit one up and sucked the smoke in deep and then coughed and coughed while my eyes and nose ran and little blue stars crawled across my visual field and I felt giddy and slack-muscled and knew that somewhere Nicotina the Tobacco Goddess was laughing at me.

I threw the cigarette away, soaking it carefully first. Chastened, I returned to my coffee. Everything tasted of salt, smoke, and metal. The brief flirtation with uncontrolled substances hadn't done anything but waste what little energy I had left.

I walked back to my desk. Slowly.

Houston wraps each of its jobs in brown paper before it sends them out. I carried seven of the books to the front of the studio. I typed out seven red-and-white labels, centering the names neatly. I wrapped each book separately in a thick, generous allotment of butcher's paper, sealed each with brown package tape, and put the nice red-and-white label on the outside. I took them back to my desk and made a cute little ziggurat of them, Glitter's on the bottom, Amyntor's on the top. Then I walked around the studio some more, barely refraining from wringing my hands.

Because Ned did not have, could not have what he'd thought he had and what I thought I'd seen. Mary, Queen of Scots, wasn't a Witch. She just *wasn't*.

*How do you know?* A serpentine inner voice asked me.

"I just do," I said out loud. Besides, whether she was Queen of Scotland or Queen of the May, the Witch she would have been would have been so different from the kind I was that we probably wouldn't recognize each other's rituals in a darkened room.

*So, nu?*

My heart was racing. Caffeine, nicotine, fear.

I went back to my desk. I opened the book again somewhere in the middle. Halfway down the crowded page there were some letters written larger. *Por Atirer en Bas La Lune.* The antique French puzzled me for some minutes, but I finally figured it out. Translated into modern and English it read:

"For Drawing Down the Moon."

The page crumbled where I held it and my fingers made a darker print on the vellum. I closed the book without trying to read any more.

Drawing down the moon. The title of a book by Margot Adler about twentieth-century Witches. The central mystery of our mystery. Say Mass and you're a priest. Draw down the moon and you're a Witch.

And everyone who'd worked at Lothlorien was dead.

I looked at my watch. It was ten-thirty; too late to bother most of the people I knew. And I didn't want to do that anyway, until I got things straight in my head.

Ned. Ilona. *The Book of Moons. Marie, la Reine de Caledonii.*

I cast my mind back over that damned book Daffydd had loaned me, chock-full of historical facts about the universe's favorite sixteenth-century queen. Okay, just suppose what I had here was what Ned thought it was. Mary Queen of Scots grimoire. No, not grimoire—Book of Shadows. *The Book of Moons* of Marie the Witch.

Just like in the ballad. Tom O'Bedlam. *The Book of Moons.*

Okay. Suppose Mary *was* an initiated Witch. Just suppose.

Where would it have been done? Scotland is a traditional haven of the Craft: Margaret Murray found scads of examples of "surviving folk belief" there in the Scots witch trial records, and even Gerald Gardner had a Scots nursemaid from whom (some say) he learned his Wicca-craeften.

And James the Sixth of Scotland (aka James the First of England)—Mary's son—was one of the most relentless anti-Witch propagandists that history records, his philippics opening the door to that sanctimonious butcher Matthew Hopkins, self-styled Witchfinder General of all England, and the bloodiest witch-hunts ever enacted on English soil.

A case of adolescent rebellion?

My mother the Witch?

Was I actually taking this *seriously?*

Why had the Berwick witches (one of Dr. Murray's prize exhibits, whose capture led to one of the most famous witch trials in history) followed the Earl of Bothwell in his plan to kill James the king? Because it would put someone sympathetic to their religion on the joint thrones of England and Scotland?

I thought about it. It was a tempting possibility. But no, if I was going to play fair with the historical facts as I knew them, Mary could not have been initiated in Scotland—she left when she was six and didn't come back until she was eighteen, and after that Knox and Moray and that lot would certainly have seized the excuse of her paganism not just to boot her out, but to *burn* her.

Not in Scotland.

In France, then. At a French court whose entire sixteenth-century existence was owed to the intercession of one of Dr. Murray's other prime candidates for Wiccanhood: Joan of Arc. *La Pucelle,* Joan the Maid. Joan the Witch. Saint Joan. Who heard voices. Who followed orders. Who collaborated in her judicial murder, to the utter confusion of friends and foes alike, at the order of—some say—the head of her coven. Some say.

If there *had* been a living French Craft tradition, it could have made the jump to the French court from the French folk, then.

I stared at *The Book of Moons.*

My speculation had now reached the outermost orbit of the supermarket press and I knew it, but I couldn't stop. Fanciful history was more palatable than factual murder.

The French court. A royal coven, headed by Catherine de Medici, perhaps, or by Dianne de Valois, the king's mistress, who raised Mary as her own daughter. What would be more reasonable, if there was a coven, than that Mary should be inducted into it?

Almost anything.

In which case, where had the book in front of me come from? A top-flight modern forgery of a sixteenth-century holograph document—which *The Book of Moons* was—took more skill than poor Ned had possessed.

So maybe it was real. Maybe. Could be. Might be.

When she returned to Scotland, Mary's lack of zeal for the Catholic faith was one of the things that made her political position so difficult. Was her indifference to the Catholic Church and her acknowledgment of the Protestants due to the fact that she herself adhered to a third faith, that of the Wicca?

Not a member of the Old Religion, as Catholicism was beginning to be called, but of the Oldest Religion?

And, banished from France, had Mary been banished from her coven as well?

And if there was a royal French coven, and she was separated from it, then Mary spent her life trying to reclaim not merely temporal glory, but spiritual.

Ridiculous. Impossible. There was no proof of the existence of organized Wicca before 1947–53, when Gardner began publishing.

I stared at the book in front of me and thought hard.

Gerald Gardner ingested all three of Murray's published revelations and on the basis of Murray's discredited scholarship proclaimed that the practice of the Craft went back centuries—at least, that's the way his critics say it happened. And once the Craft developed a more broad-based demographic, people with credible scholarly training attempted to climb the Wiccan family tree and found nothing before Gardner. From all the evidence they have been able to gather, what we know as Wicca began with Gerald Gardner.

What would they give for concrete real-world proof that it did not? That it was, in fact, a centuries-old religion?

I shook my head, driving the cobwebs out. If this was real, if it involved Mary, it was much bigger than that. If she could drive people like Daffydd and Beaner crazy after four hundred years of being dead when she was just an unlucky Catholic queen, imagine what her being a Witch would do.

I looked at *The Book of Moons*. Where had it come

from—and what was I going to do with it? It wasn't mine to dispose of. It wasn't Ned's either, it was safe to say, but whose was it?

Whoever the book belonged to, I didn't have to worry about it tonight. I was so tired I could hardly keep my eyes open, and almost anything I did would be sure to be wrong.

So I wrapped it up the way I had the other eight, typed "Book of Moons" on the label, and put it with the rest of my new collection of purloined Books of Shadows. At least this way I wouldn't lose it.

Then I locked up the studio and walked home, a habit I'm going to pay for some night, I know.

But not this one.

# 7

**H**aving been so reasonable and prudent, I didn't get much sleep after all.

I lay in bed and stared at the ceiling and thought about Ned and *The Book of Moons.* I thought about what intervention I could have made in Ned's life to have given it a different outcome. I wondered if he'd be alive if I'd taken a taxi, if I'd listened to him more, if I'd encouraged Belle to take him into Changing.

And I knew I wouldn't have done those things. I hadn't had any telegram from the future telling me what Ned would turn rejection into—and if I had, what then? This was the dark side of the possession of power: knowing the pain it caused people like Ned, who somehow, by some standard, weren't good enough.

Pain that could, in the end, kill.

If the Craft is all smoke and mirrors—if it is merely the recreation of ignoble minds—then there is no justification for all of the pain that it causes.

But if instead it is not a faith, but a practicum inspired by gnosis and observation of the noumenal world, then the pain is, if not justified, in some sense pardonable. Pardonable because mere comfort cannot be the human animal's highest good. If it is, Nature, daughter of the Goddess, is made unnatural, since She has overfitted Her creatures for this world.

These were not comfortable thoughts to spend the night with. But comfort, as I have said, is not the goal.

And in that much we had made Ned a part of the Craft after all, because he had found no comfort with us.

Seven A.M. I thought about calling in dead, but I needed the hours. Besides, the books were at the studio. I had to return them before something else happened to them. So I dragged myself out of bed and took a shower, drank three cups of coffee, dug out and emptied the Danish Bookbag, and went.

It was still cool on the street, cooler—in fact—than it was indoors. I stopped at the deli and bought replacement cigarettes for Eloi and coffee for me and went up to the studio.

"You left the coffeepot on last night," Ray said when I came in.

I groaned and looked around for Mikey.

"He isn't here yet. I put it to soak," Ray said, relenting. "You look like hell. You got those dies done yet?"

"Soon," I said. "Patience is a virtue," I added.

Ray sneered. He's very good at it.

I went and washed out the coffeepot in the sink by the stat camera. I went back and made fresh coffee. Royce and Seiko were here, but most of the carrels were empty: no work, so no Angela and Tyrell and Eloi and Chantal.

I took four Excedrin for that run-down feeling and put extra sugar in my coffee from the deli. Then, feeling nauseated and slightly buzzed, I finished the jobs for Ray and meticulously cleaned my area. I made two brief phone calls on the studio phone: Glitter was in, Belle was not. Around noon I put the binding die mechanicals on Ray's desk.

"You got anything else for me?" I said.

"Go home. Sleep. You look horrible," Ray said. "I'll see you tomorrow."

Which meant he didn't.

"Yeah," I said. I bundled seven wrapped parcels into the bookbag and left.

It is an amazing truth of the universe that people always feel better the moment they leave work. For example, I almost felt as though I'd managed to get some sleep. I took the 6 downtown and got off at the City Hall station.

Glitter works in the big building on Court Street. The lobby is black and white marble, and in addition to bearing a generic resemblance to postwar buildings of a certain age, has always struck me as being a facade of tidiness slapped over some of the bleaker functioning of our society. Magical thinking: if you don't see it, it isn't there.

I gave my destination to a guard and took an elevator and gave my name to another guard who called into the back to see if I was expected. Glitter came out and conducted me into her office.

The place where Glitter does her probation officering for the City of New York is a glass-walled cubicle with a glass door, WPA vintage. It's about eight by ten, and where it isn't glass it is painted gas-chamber green. It contains two file cabinets, two chairs, a coatrack, and a desk, also green. The cubicle walls do not go all the way up to the ceiling. The back wall, above the height of the cubicle, is a dark brown-black and covered with exposed ductwork. The blackness does go all the way up.

"So, you want to go to lunch?" Glitter said. She was wearing tiers and layers of hand-painted lavender-rose chiffon, spangled with fugitive rhinestones. Her pumps were a violent purple.

I took a deep breath. "I got something back for you, but I don't want to talk about it yet, okay?"

I handed her the package. She knew what it was the moment she touched it, but tore at it until she'd opened a corner of the wrapping just to be sure. Purple lamé showed.

"It's my book," Glitter said in an airless voice. She stared at me, open-mouthed, and then at the neat burden of similar parcels in my bag. She sat down behind her desk, clutching her book. After a moment she collected herself and put it into her bottom drawer.

"Ned Skelton got whacked last night," she said. "Maura told me, 'cause I knew him. He'd come to my place a couple times. With Ilona, you know? He wanted to join a group. I was the one who told Belle about him."

I waited. I couldn't see where this conversation was going. *Whacked?*

"It was a very professional job," Glitter went on. "Close up and a little gun. .22 or .25, they think. Right at the back of the head."

I didn't think I wanted to hear this.

"And we all heard Ned at the picnic," Glitter said, talking to the top of her desk. She threw up her hands. "Oh my god, I can't do this!"

I finally saw where the conversation was going. I sat down, feeling as if she'd punched me.

"You think Ned stole your book." Which, as a matter of fact, he had, but never mind. "You think I killed him to get it back?" This was far stupider and more unfair. My voice rose indignantly.

"No, no, no." Glitter waved her hands very fast. "Just took something from the crime scene where you maybe were. That's all. For Goddess's sake, Bast, I don't think you'd *kill* somebody!"

*Probably* hung heavy in the air. Sometimes I wonder what my enemies think of me, considering the opinions my friends have.

"Glitter, you are a wonderful human being, but— go. Write novels," I said. "Have a rich, full, emotional life."

I could have explained it all—the package Ned asked me to hold (for the receipt of which I, comfortingly, had witnesses), the phone call, the ruined city and fair Helen dead, but I didn't want to tell her about any part of last night. Glitter is an officer of the court, and while she is flexible about most things, she isn't about some things. If I actually had to talk to the police, I wanted to do it on my own initiative.

She sat back. "Sorry," she muttered. "It's this job. You look for reasons. And there aren't any. But where—"

"I can't tell you that," I said. I wasn't sure why. Damage control. Or maybe I was trying to gear myself up for a career of outlawry.

"So, lunch?" Glitter said finally, after I hadn't said anything for a while.

I shrugged, a woman of few words and many gestures. "Some things to do," I said. "I'll see you later."

She walked me out. There were the tenderings of explanations in my future—I could see that—but just now, the way I had last night, I was buying time.

I wasn't quite sure why. But I knew there were things I had to do before the reckoning came.

There's one place where all the lines of communication in the Community cross: the Snake—or rather, the Snake's manager. Julian.

Julian is a ritual magician, a scholar of magic and its history, and one of the more closemouthed people alive. This does not mean that he does not hear things. As if to Rick's Café Americain, everybody eventually comes to the Snake.

And Julian would know whose books these were and how to return them. If I was lucky, he'd even leave my name out of it.

I got up to the Snake around one o'clock and was glad to see the store was open—the Snake's hours tend to be rather whimsical. I passed under the neon sign, slid around the blessedly silent Elvis jukebox (it was blocking the doorway even more than usual), and walked in. As far as the naked eye could see, the place was deserted.

The shop smelled resinously of burned incense; a haze of frankincense hung in the air like a set-dressing special effect. I looked around and spotted the source in front of the Snake's ecumeni-altar, the one that started life as a birdbath that'd had a heavy date with *Primavera*. The shell part is usually full of pennies (this being a retail establishment) or flowers. Today it was full of hot charcoal and about half a pound of expensive resin busily transforming itself into blue smoke. I went on, past the case full of crystal balls and ancient Egyptian meteorites and genuine Lady of the Lake chalices. The Siege Perilous was deserted, and something about that nagged at me, even in my current preoccupied state.

I had the growing conviction that I was being led down the garden path, round Robin Hood's barn, and up to a conclusion I was supposed to jump from without understanding. In short, I had the feeling that my subconscious mind knew what was going on and I didn't.

I hate that.

I was halfway down the right aisle when I saw the secret bookcase swing out. I nipped around the end of the rack and surprised Julian coming out of the back room. He had an open book in one hand and looked like a pensive divine. He glanced up and saw me. The corners of his mouth quirked upward ever so slightly.

"I suppose you know why I'm here," I said, which was not what I'd meant to say.

"You've come to see our new look?" Julian said blandly.

I looked appropriately puzzled. The bag on my shoulder was getting heavier. Julian watched me not get it, and finally explained.

"Somebody tried to break into the Snake last night," he said.

Religious tolerance and the gentle art of minding one's own business being what they are, the Snake receives an average of one editorial declaration per week from people who just can't bear its existence one moment longer. More, if you count the phone threats.

These declarations range from pamphlets advocating the religion of your choice stuffed in the door, to bricks and bullets aimed at the window. The window has been replaced twice—to the best of my knowledge—in the time I've been going to the Snake.

I followed Julian up to the front of the shop.

We got to the front door. Julian pushed the jukebox back, and I saw what it had been hiding.

He'd lied.

*Tried* to break in was not truth in advertising.

Whoever it was that had paid the Serpent's Truth a visit last night had gotten the padlock off the outside gate and then gone after the door with a wood chisel. There were long flat gouges all down the red-over-green-over-blue-over-white paint, but those were only hesitation marks, really. Eventually whoever it was had found his angle, and there were deep, competent cuts into the door around the lock-plate exposing new white wood. It looked like performance art by Beavers With Attitude.

"The alarm went off and the service called me and then Tris, but—" Julian shrugged. "At least they didn't do too much damage."

"What did they get?" I asked, before I could stop myself. The urge to meddle is strong, even though I've never done myself any good by it yet.

"They went straight for the grimoires," Julian said.

I looked up at the locked glass case behind the cash register and Julian's Siege Perilous, where the really, *really* expensive part of the Snake's inventory is kept. Most of it is first or rare editions of occult books—like an 1801 edition of Francis Barrett's *The Magus* with marginalia, or a signed copy of *White Stains*—but sometimes a limited-run tarot deck or a piece of jewelry will be added to the collection.

It wasn't there.

I realized why the front of the shop had looked so odd to me when I came in. No cabinet.

It was on the floor, propped against the wall. The doors of the cabinet had been sheared cleanly off, leaving small whorls of pale splinters where the hinges had used to be. The shelves, usually jammed, were bare.

I would say that the contents of that one cabinet represent about fifteen to twenty-five thousand dollars of the Snake's total inventory.

"Damn," I said. "I'm sorry."

"That's life in the big city," Julian said. "Someone went on a spree. Weiser's and Mirror Mirror were hit up, too."

Weiser's, Mirror Mirror, and the Snake are all occult bookstores. They are also the only three occult bookstores in New York that have a rare books section.

"Last night," I said. Julian nodded once.

Which gave Ned Skelton the best alibi anyone ever had, not that he needed it. The BoS thefts had been done by someone who knew the Community pretty well, who laughed at locks and went through them as if they weren't there. He did not chop his way in with an ax.

It wasn't—I dredged up terminology from my leisure reading—it wasn't the same M.O., even if it had the same sort of Wonderland illogic to it as Ned's had.

For example, who would break into the Snake and not even smash anything? When Chanter's Revel, a feminist Wicca store in the East Village, got tossed last year the burglars didn't take anything, but they totaled all the merchandise they could get their hands on.

Here, they'd only stolen the rare books. Why?

It wasn't for their arcane secrets; almost everything in that case was available as cheap reprints.

It wasn't for the money; you couldn't resell those books for anything like what they'd cost retail. If it was a straightforward robbery for gain, why had they taken the books and left the gold and silver jewelry? If they had—but Julian'd said they went "straight for the grimoires," and the jewelry cases looked typically cluttered.

I wondered if the pattern was the same at Weiser's and Mirror Mirror.

"What are you going to do?" I asked Julian.

"Call the insurance company. Prove what we paid for them. Get half of it back." Julian shrugged and shoved the jukebox back into place. He looked strange in the afternoon sunlight; Julian is a creature of night and shadows.

I recalled finally that I had another purpose for being here.

"Would you do something for me?" I asked Julian. *Like help me get some stolen property back to its rightful owners.*

I knew he did this sort of thing because I'd had it done for me once. Or maybe *to* me would be more accurate.

Julian stopped looking at the door and looked at me.

"There are some packages," I said carefully, "that I would like to see get to their proper destinations. I think most of the recipients come in here."

I waited. Julian waited. Or maybe he was thinking. He turned away and stepped up to the Siege Perilous. He quirked a finger and I followed him.

The reason that the Siege Perilous is raised up is so that the person sitting at it can clearly see both aisles and most of the rest of the retail floor of the store. I regarded the empty aisles and swung my carryall up onto the table. I pulled out the books.

Julian sorted through them. He piled Xharina's and Amyntor's and Lorelli's brown-paper-wrapped books in one corner. He hesitated over Crystal, then piled her and Otterleaf and Diana-27 in a second pile.

"I don't know them," Julian said, which meant you'd have to go a long way to find anyone who did.

"Any clues?" I said. "Crystal works Faery in Fort Lee. Otterleaf's a Gardnerian."

His brow cleared. He retrieved Crystal's package and wrote "Doreen" on it with a large soft pencil, then added it to the first pile. I was touched at the special effort he was making for me, or possibly he felt that all those good customers and true would show their gratitude at these returns by overspending.

"You can find Otterleaf yourself," Julian said reprovingly, which was true, although it'd probably mean going to Freya.

Freya is Belle's Queen—the woman who brought her into the Craft—a very public woman from a very public family who manages to avoid most of the woo-woo associated with the public profession of Wicca and Goddess-worship by simply being far too cool for anyone to ask her stupid questions. She's also almost never home.

"Yeah, right," I said.

I put the two he hadn't ID'd—Otterleaf's and Diana-27's—back into my bag. Belle might be able to place both of them and get the books back to them, but then again she'd probably tell their recipients where she'd gotten them, Belle being incurably forthright and a rebuke to us all.

While Julian loved nothing more than mystery, and would probably delight in keeping my name out of things.

I shouldn't like that, but I do.

"Anything else?" Julian asked. He sounded like the chief devil in a Restoration farce.

*Why did someone break in here after grimoires? Is it tied to Ilona's death? Here, and Weiser's, and Mirror Mirror are the only three places in the city that stock antique occult books, and whoever it was hit all three. How did he know? What is he after? Do you know who he is? Would you tell me if you did?*

"No. Nothing," I said.

Wednesday. Two-forty-five. I made it up the stairs and behind my own locks alive, which is a triumph of a sort here in Fun City. And every year it gets harder.

Twentieth-century occult thought holds that the major population centers are a generation ahead of the rest of the world—or, what New York is now, Tulsa, Oklahoma, will be in twenty years.

Makes you long to see what 2015'll be like at Fourth Street and Sixth, doesn't it?

I tried Belle again. She was still out. Which was annoying, considering how much I wanted to talk to her.

It's not that I run to Belle with every little thing. But this was not a little thing. This was theft—crazy, extensive, and stupid. It might even be connected to murder, an explicit, real-world murder that our friends the police were even now investigating. I wanted to know what she thought, what she knew, what she'd heard.

I wanted to shove the responsibility onto someone else so that I wasn't even a psychic accessory-be-side-the-fact to Ned Skelton's life. Backward, turn backward, O time in thy flight. But childhood was a long time gone.

My apartment was airless, but not yet an oven. I got the fan down from where it lives the rest of the year and propped it in the window and turned it on, facing out. Air began sliding through.

*From the hag and hungry goblin, that into rags would rend ye / All the spirits that stand by the Naked Man in The Book of Moons defend ye.*

I stretched out on the bed, tried to think about *The Book of Moons*, and fell asleep.

The phone woke me. It was hours later, and the temperature had dropped to where I was shivering. I hoped it was Belle calling back, but it wasn't. I picked up anyway as the caller began leaving a message.

"Hi, Stuart," I said, just as if I were a normal person.

"Hello," he said. His voice was sultry and edged, like good Scotch. "I was wondering if you'd care to have dinner with me this evening?"

*Oh, Jesus, no!* my mind said, while my mouth said, "Sure, Stuart, that'd be great." I regarded the phone with the horrified feeling you have when the car's front wheels leave the paving, but it transmitted my words without editorial comment.

"That's lovely, then," Stuart said. "Why don't we meet somewhere and go on from there? What about the Russian Tea Room?"

I laughed out of sheer nerves, though he couldn't know why I found the suggestion funny. "I'm off things Russian," I said, feeling all my old heterosexual diplomacy skills come raging back. My turn to curtsey, your turn to bow.

"Top of the Sixes, then?" he said.

I blinked. According to the formal Rules of Engagement that govern dating, if you decline the first suggestion made for where to go you have to accept the second one, since two refusals imply lack of interest.

But the Top of the Sixes is an authentic New York Legend located at 666 Fifth Avenue and has commanded a panoramic top-floor view of New York City for lo these many years. It is expensive. Very, very expensive. Either Stuart had been struck independently wealthy or was expecting more out of this evening than I thought he was going to get.

I mentally reviewed my wardrobe, wondering if I even owned anything I could wear there. Nothing to wear was a valid justification for negotiation.

"Sweetheart?"

"Huh? I mean sure, great. When?" Why was my mouth doing this to me?

"Perhaps an hour?"

"Oh, yeah, fine, sure," I said, with the immense suavity that characterizes my dealings with real grown-ups.

Stuart swore he was looking forward to seeing me and also to a delightful evening, which I thought was more optimism than the English are generally credited with. I put the phone down and stared at it.

I'd agreed to go out on a date to the Top of the Sixes with a man I'd barely met and hardly knew. I ran a quick sanity check and found all systems stable.

I realized that I was going to enjoy this evening. It would be the tonic antithesis of murdered booksellers, *The Book of Moons,* and all the byzantine Community politics that were beginning to grate on my nerves. It would be awkward and tense, possibly expensive, almost certainly mortifying in spots, and would leave me feeling massively incapable of coping with the innocent social interactions of our culture.

It would also be normal. Supremely normal. It was a date, a thing that everybody did—people who had never heard of the Goddess or Mary, Queen of Scots, people who had never known someone who'd been killed, people who had never been handed a dead man's legacy to return, people who owned televisions and didn't live in a coffin-shaped and coffin-sized apartment on the edge of Alphabet City.

People who owned suitable clothing for the occasion.

I got up, shoved my hair out of my eyes, and went to my closet.

I own any number of clothing items, including skirts (most in basic black), but only two dresses: the Laura Ashley print that makes me look like an escapee from a Burne-Jones painting and a lined black linen sheath that unfortunately does not make me look like Audrey Hepburn but does allow me to state truthfully that I have a dress from Sak's, even if bought on sale. I could also field an envelope clutch and shoes that matched each other and the dress.

Fine.

Half an hour later I was standing in front of my mirror smudging my eye sockets in with expensive *grisalle* powder the purchase of which (if not the use) is one of my few unjustifiable vices, realizing that I owned no jewelry that went with the dress and that if I spent much more time worrying about it I was going to be late. I left the silver studs in my back piercings and put big silver crescents in the front ones and decided I was understatedly elegant. Time to go.

Wearing a dress in my neighborhood made me feel vulnerable and out of place, as though I were somehow out of contact with the ground. I decided on yet another in a series of taxis, but they don't come down into my locality much. I walked across the Bowery and got lucky, snagging one cruising Lower Broadway. I got to Top of the Sixes a little after seven.

I did not belong here. The sense of inappropriateness was as seductive as a drug.

The first thing you see when you walk into Top of the Sixes is a wall of glass looking out over the city.

Sunset turns every visible window into a mirror flashing back gold sunset light, and down below the streets are already in shadow, even though the sky is light. It's a stage set, meant for after the theater, for later evening, for someone I wasn't and didn't want to be.

But the power to be this far from my proper place was, all side issues aside, power. And, as Lord Acton said, power delights, and absolute power is absolutely delightful.

I was not in a harmless mind-set.

The wait-staff elicited the information that I was waiting for someone, which seemed, somehow, to relieve them. I was installed on a real leather end stool in front of an intimidating sweep of mirror and mahogany, where I allowed a bartender to pour me a Scotch on the rocks for seven-fifty. I set my purse on the edge of the bar and felt that someone ought to offer to light the cigarette I wasn't smoking. Ah, expectation.

I sat and read the labels on the expensive booze and admired the pretheater diners and the collection of people who thought nothing of coming to the Top of the Sixes for a drink before dinner and marveled at the infinite diversity of human society. How lovely it is to have money, as the song goes.

It was a good thing that I found so much to amuse myself with, because Stuart didn't make an appearance. Seven-thirty became eight. I ordered another drink and tried not to feel the twitch from that old bad girly-girl hardwiring: *he* boots it and it's *your* fault. Prepackaged inferiority.

But he *had* said Top of the Sixes and he *had* said seven. I sat there, giddy with disrupted sleep patterns and emotional dressage and the sublimated terror of unconnectedness. Possibly everyone else felt this way all the time. Maybe that was why they were here. Maybe that was why all of twentieth-century culture was here.

*And what about Mary Stuart?* my mind demanded.

I wasn't surprised to be thinking of her. It's like that old Discordian koan: "All things happen in fives, or are divisible by or are multiples of five, or are somehow directly or indirectly appropriate to five . . . depending on the ingenuity of the observer."

Mary was my five. Mary, Mary, quite contrary, who, if she *was* a Witch, knew when she went to the block that her co-religionists had abandoned her, the latest in a long series of abandonments, jiltings, and betrayals.

Speaking of which—

At eight-forty-five I decided that Stuart had either stood me up or been unavoidably delayed, and I wasn't going to invest any emotion in either possibility until I found out which it was. We are all so modern and reasonable here at the end of the millennium.

I settled the bill and got ready to go. So far the evening was living up to expectations—embarrassing and expensive. Nobody paid any attention to me, but then, nobody would. This is New York's great gift to the neurotic: anonymity.

I'm not neurotic, but I try to keep up with my friends' interests.

It was dark outside; the place looked less surreal. There are things meant to be seen only in darkness that exist, anticlimactically, in the light of day. Like Julian.

Who I was supposed to be banishing from my consciousness with this little exercise.

I returned to the elevator. It opened. I recognized Stuart before he recognized me.

"What— Good heavens, sweetheart, I didn't even see you!"

He was wearing a suit and tie, which added to my sense of unreality. I don't know people who dress like that.

"Hello, Stuart," I said. "You're late," I added.

He looked cross that I'd mentioned it and contrite all at the same time, which was amusing, but probably not amusing enough to make me continue the evening any further.

"Oh, you poor girl—you must be starved. Come on, let's go get dinner. Give me a chance to explain. There's a little place around the corner."

He took my arm. I didn't like it but I didn't object. My mistake.

The technical name for Stuart's little maneuver is bait and switch, but the consolation prize was hushed and elegant, three blocks away, and so self-effacing and dimly lit that I wasn't quite sure what its name was. The decor seemed to run to polished copper implements, leather, and wooden ducks in various states of preservation. We were ushered directly to a booth, suggesting that this was where Stuart had been heading all along. Leather menus the size of solar panels were tendered unto us. I discovered that the restaurant's name was Sandalford's and the entrées started at $22.50. Stuart asked me what I was drinking.

"Perrier with a chunk," I said, feeling it would not be a good idea to send a third Scotch to live with the other two just yet. Stuart ordered a double Bushmill's, no ice. His shirt had French cuffs and his cufflinks were gold lions' heads. Very fancy. I wondered if they were Scottish lions.

"You must think I'm a perfectly dreadful person," Stuart said charmingly, in a fashion that encouraged me to disagree.

"Not yet," I said.

I am not easily charmed. Neither am I anyone's sweetheart, baby, darling, or poor girl, which you may consider a moral failing on my part, if you like. Stuart was oh-so-subtly pushing me around— manipulating me, if you prefer—a practice of which I disapprove.

"I tried to reach you, but you'd already left," he said. Winsomely. There was something underneath the winsomeness, some dark current of self-congratulation that interested me; I'm not trophy enough that possession of me would engender it. "I was just about to pop out the door myself when *les gendarmes* appeared upon the horizon." He raised his eyebrows, inviting sympathy.

"What?" I said blankly.

"The police," Stuart amplified. He shrugged. "I'd already told them everything I know, but apparently something new had come up and things had changed." He finished his drink and called for another with a practiced flick of the finger. "I don't mind telling you, I'm quite at the end of my tether. What a horror."

"You had to talk to the police," I said, wondering if I'd heard him correctly.

"Well, of course," Stuart said. "Ilona was my aunt; they usually want to talk to the family. I'd ask you to the funeral, but I'm having the body shipped home, and—"

I was suddenly far beyond sober, in the nauseated nightmare realm of three A.M. awakenings poisoned with adrenaline, among jagged annunciations that it takes years of practice to learn not to reject.

Stuart was Ilona's nephew.

Ilona had been supposed to come to the picnic on Sunday with her nephew, her new partner.

But Stuart had come alone, with never a mention about Ilona to me or anyone else.

Why?

If she'd been alive, he would have brought her. If she couldn't come, he would have made her excuses. Ilona was a lady of the old school. She had manners. She would have sent her regrets.

If she were alive.

If she was dead, what kind of lunatic would register that fact and then go on to his next social engagement?

Ilona had died sometime Saturday night. She'd been going to bring him to the picnic; they would have met at her place or his. He must have known she was dead, all the time I was talking to him that Sunday.

What kind of lunatic . . . ?

"Bast, darling, are you all right? You look a bit illish," Stuart said.

"Bad drug reaction," I said automatically. The fresh drink arrived.

"Look, I can't go on calling you by that ridiculous name," Stuart said. "You must have a real name somewhere." He put his hand over mine and I realized he was trying to pry my purse out of my fingers. "Let's see what it is." Playfully.

"I suppose Lothlorien is yours now," I said, tightening my fingers on my purse.

"Yes, of course," Stuart said, letting go of my hand. "The will has yet to be proved, but as far as I know I'm her only relative; in fact, she'd asked me to became a partner in that bookstore of hers. I don't know what I'll do with the place. Sell the books, I expect. I suppose they're worth a bit."

"In the right market," I said. My brain was occupied with how to get out of here before I asked Stuart why he'd killed Ilona.

And Ned. The killer of one had to be the killer of the other, because he was after *The Book of Moons.*

Because it was worth a lot of money and it was an old family heirloom and Ilona had been going to sell an old family heirloom to finance Lothlorien but Ned had stolen *The Book of Moons* just like he'd stolen all the other Books of Shadows—

And I had *The Book of Moons* now.

"I know it sounds rather callous and mercenary of me to be reckoning up pounds-shillings-pence so soon, but I hadn't seen her in years, really," Stuart said.

"Excuse me," I said to Stuart. I stood up. He stood up. I fled.

\*   \*   \*

The bathroom at Sandalford's is pink and extensive, with decor dropped down from another manqué: black and pink with glazed and sandblasted lilies, savagely retro and antiseptic. I looked in the mirror and saw a scared raccoon, painted and blue-eyed, teetering on the edge of cobbling together a real-world explanation for her terror, denying the fact that it was a reasonable response to the acquisition of information she could not possibly possess.

I was certain of Stuart's accountability in the murders, even while I shied away and tried to find alternative justifications for my feelings.

I was just spooked at going out on a date. Sure.

No. There was something wrong here. But if I clung to my conviction of Stuart Hepburn's homicide I'd simply talk myself out of it and walk back out onto the killing floor.

I took a deep breath and closed my eyes. What was wrong? Don't ask for specifics: magic is an analog system, not digital. I breathed deeply and sorted through my last half hour with Stuart. Something wrong. Forget murder. Cool premeditated murder was too grandiose to easily believe in.

But violence was not. There was something odd, unreasonable, unreal, forced, faked in Stuart's behavior. Something that didn't fit into the continuum of two casual meetings and the suggestion of dinner.

Stuart was setting me up.

I did not have to believe he'd killed two people to accept that warning. His character fault might be something as mundane and ugly as a taste for date rape. I didn't have to stay to find out what it was. The only question remaining was how to leave.

People die every year from the fear of looking stupid. At least when you're a Witch you have enough experience at looking stupid that you know it won't, of itself, kill you.

I walked back out to the table. Stuart stood up.

"I've already ordered," he said. "When you didn't come back, I—"

"Stuart," I said, interrupting. "This is not working out. I'm sorry about the police, but I'm leaving now. Good-bye."

He grabbed for my arm, but there was a table between us and I was expecting it. I moved fast, aceing the restaurant traffic with elite New York pedestrian chops. Stuart was tangled with waiters and explanations, unable to follow.

I reached the outside air and ran down the first subway steps I saw.

It took me a while to get out of the area and to transfer to a line going somewhere I wanted to go, and by that time it was as easy to take the Uptown A as it was to do anything else.

By now it was rising ten. So far today I'd been accused of murder by Glitter, conspired in occult psychodrama with Julian, taken a fling at being a yuppie and spent twenty dollars for two Scotches at Top of the Sixes, and almost had dinner with the real murderer.

Now that I was away from him I could go back to believing it, and the more I thought about it, the more it all made a horrible Agatha Christie kind of sense.

All it took was one leap of unproven faith: that Ilona Saunders, expatriate Brit, had *The Book of*

*Moons,* a family heirloom, the (reluctantly chosen) sale of which was going to save Lothlorien.

Maybe she consulted with Stuart about selling it. He'd said she'd offered him a partnership. I wondered with a sudden intense yearning for knowledge what it was that Stuart did for his day job that allowed him to possess those lovely suits and gold cufflinks and familiarity with posh eateries. The proceeds form the sale of *The Book of Moons* could enhance a lifestyle like that: make it possible, or make its continuation possible.

But when the time came to show *The Book of Moons* to her nephew and new partner, Stuart Hepburn, Ilona didn't have it. Because Ned Skelton, her part-time clerk, whose other job it was to go in and out of strangers' apartments with his set of master passkeys, had branched out, entering many apartments and carefully removing from each an item that was valueless except to the Witch who had written it—or to someone who desperately wanted the moral validity that being Wiccan would give him: the Books of Shadows.

So Ned stole Ilona's book among his other thefts. *The Book of Moons.* Mary's book. The one thing that tied all of this together: the McGuffin, without which, as the saying goes, one cannot hunt tigers in Scotland.

The subway arrived at my destination. I crossed Dyckman. Belle had better be home this time.

Belle's apartment is on the fifth floor of an end building overlooking High Bridge Park, and the landlord has been intermittently trying to get her to move out for years. The place has four bedrooms, no furniture to speak of, and a door chime and sound system courtesy of The Cat, whose motto is Better Living Through Technology.

My shoes made wounded gazelle rhythms across the lobby and up five flights of stairs. The doorbell's selection this month sampled the "Mars Movement" from Holst's *The Planets* as played on the glocken-spiel. I leaned on it for awhile. Eventually Belle came to the peephole.

"Bast?" she said, as if there were hundreds of people out there in Fun City impersonating me.

"Yeah," I said. "I need to tell you something."

Normal people use the phone, or E-mail, or at least don't come banging on other people's doors at eleven o'clock at night unannounced. Belle is used to the differently normal. She let me in. She did not say, "What are you got up as?" because Belle's accep-tance is all-encompassing.

She was wearing a yellow terry-cloth bathrobe, a garment that makes her look like an enormous baby chicken. She went to put on tea. The kitchen light was the only light in the apartment.

I wandered around the living room. There were seashells and crystals and candles on the window-sills, a "lives alone with no cats" clutter. Belle doesn't have any living room curtains, and in the dark her collection of colored suncatchers looked dull against the glass. A car swung up Riverside, and in the shine of its headlights I saw that it had started to rain.

I sat down on Belle's emotional rescue couch, the piece of furniture on which more Pagan New Yorkers have had crises than any other. The light from the kitchen made a yellowish trapezoid against the bare wood floor.

Belle came in and sat down next to me. "Glitter called me," she said.

"Ned gave me a box to hold for him," I said. "Look, do you still know that guy in the police?"

"Lieutenant Hodiac?" Belle said.

One of Belle's outreach functions is being Wicca advisor to the police. As far as I can determine, this involves going downtown and identifying pieces of jewelry and photographs of strange designs about four times a year and sorting out the difference between Wicca and rock music in the police mind.

"Whoever," I said.

"Bast, what are you—?" Belle said.

"I'm losing my last marble. Look. This is not a good day. I need to tell you a story, and then you tell me what I do with it."

"Okay," Belle said, looking worried. She went and got the tea, and some cookies that were still left over from the picnic. I took one and was about to bite it until I remembered that Ned had brought cookies that day and maybe these were those. I set it back down and sipped my tea.

"Ilona Saunders and Ned Skelton are dead," I said, as carefully specific as if I were arguing a case. "You remember what happened at the picnic; Ned's announcement and all. The next day I heard Ilona was dead, and then—the same day—Ned asked me to hold a package for him. That was Monday.

"Tuesday night around five-thirty he called and told me he'd been burgled Monday late sometime. He wanted a banishing ritual done on the place, you know? I left right away, but by the time I got there they were putting him into the ambulance. Shot dead, Glitter said today. In the back of the head with something small."

Belle put her hand over mine. I held it.

"What was in the box?" she said.

"Books. Books of Shadows. All the ones he stole. Glitter's. Everyone's. He was a building super; he had passkeys for all the standard locks. He asked me not to open it, or ask what was in it, but he was dead so I did. I've got—"

I realized that I didn't have Diana-27 and Otter-leaf's books with me. "There are two of them I need your help to get back to their owners."

"And he left the box with you on Monday?" Belle said.

"What, you think he did it Tuesday after he died?" I snapped. I let go of her hand. I drank my tea and jittered.

"I'm just trying to figure out what's going on here and how I can help," Belle said soothingly.

"What's going on is I almost had dinner with the guy who clocked both him and Ilona and the reason he did it is sitting in my studio." I stood up. I wandered. I leaned against the windowsill. "I'm trying to make a straight story out of this," I complained, "and it keeps getting all tangled up."

"Just tell it any way you need to. You seem awfully upset," Belle said.

My HPS, the mistress of tactful understatement.

"He must have started doing it in April. Maybe Glitter's was the first, and then when we didn't call him to join Changing he stole all the others. Ned. I heard about it at the picnic—the missing books, I mean. *That* there were missing books," I amplified

carefully. "Glitter was right all along. She didn't lose
it, she didn't misplace it. Ned took it. He went up to
Glitter's apartment with Ilona for dinner, and he
came back and took it. They knew each other: you
gave him the look-see because Glitter asked you to.
That's why you asked me to dinner instead of her—
she couldn't be objective."

Belle nodded. I came back and sat down, feeling
my way through the explanation.

"Ned was stealing Books of Shadows because he
wanted to be a Witch and nobody'd initiate him. Apparently he'd been around the track a couple of
times: Reisha, Maidjene, Xharina, Lorelli—he'd
worked with plenty of people in the Community and
nobody'd give him a tumble. He knew where they
lived; he went in on his keys and got their books—
only he didn't think of himself as a thief; he didn't
take anything else. He stole their books," I repeated,
"but that didn't get him what he really wanted." I
held up a hand, just as if Belle were about to inter-
rupt, which she wasn't.

"But then—I'm guessing, but it all fits—he took
something out of Lothlorien. *The Book of Moons.*"

Belle frowned disbelievingly.

"Ask Beaner," I said. "The building'd been sold,
her rent'd been raised, she was going to have to go,
except she told us she was going to buy the building.
She could afford to, she said, because she'd made up
her mind to sell an old family heirloom. *The Book of
Moons*—Mary, Queen of Scots's, Book of Shadows."

Damned, doomed, dazzled Mary—whose bare
name, four centuries later, caused people to turn off
their common sense.

"Bast," Belle said patiently, "if a major historical figure had been a Witch, we'd know. You don't believe—"

"Money," I said.

Belle looked at me.

"I have seen this book," I enunciated clearly. "It can be one of three things. It can be real, it can be a forgery of the period, or it can be a modern forgery. If it is modern, it is a good enough fake to be taken for old, which means it is worth money. Hitler-diaries money. Jack-the-Ripper diaries money—and it doesn't matter if both of those were faked; they were front-page news and million-dollar auctions. Enough to buy full-bore Manhattan real estate. Forget Mary. I don't care what *The Book of Moons* really is. It doesn't matter what it really is, when what it is, is money."

Belle sighed, and I realized then that I'd lost her. Maybe it was unfair of me to want her to believe on my bare say-so, when I'd had all the days since the picnic and the chance to hold *The Book of Moons* in my hands to help convince me.

That, and seeing Stuart's eyes.

"Maybe it sounds unlikely. But it's true."

Belle sighed. "I know *you* think of it as true," she said, trying to be kind.

That hurt. Belle looked at me and then padded off to the kitchen. She came back with a glass full of wine that looked like grape jelly and tasted (I knew from experience) like cough syrup. I set it down untasted.

Elitism is the stalking horse of American culture. Critics are automatically elitists, beginning the moment they say that something is better than something else. In our headlong rush to throw down an aristocracy that has not existed in two centuries, we avow hysterically that everything is not only as good as everything else, but *is*, in fact, everything else.

But when everything is everything, how do you define anything?

I didn't want to be the only one to see things the way I saw them. No one is that secure. But I wasn't going to say I didn't see them, either.

*"She would not say she was not married when she was."* Catherine of Aragon. Another queen, another adjudicated destruction. Paths of glory lead only to the grave.

"Where is this book now?" Belle asked finally.

"Wrapped up like the others, sitting at the studio," I said, forgetting that Diana-27's and Otterleaf's were at my apartment. "But you aren't interested in my theories. I'm sorry I bothered you."

The more I thought about Belle's remark—mild, really—the angrier I got. Either because it was true, or because she thought it was true, or because I needed to be angry.

"Who'd you get all dressed up for?" Belle asked.

"Stuart Hepburn." I stood up. "The man who killed Ilona Saunders and Ned Skelton. For the book. For money."

"What makes you say that?"

She was treating me like a patient; standing back and reserving judgment. But I hadn't come here for that. I'd come for a partisan, a friend, someone who believed the things I did.

But I already knew she didn't.

I'd thought we'd patched up our friendship. I'd thought things were going to be the same between us. I knew that Belle'd thought so too.

We'd both been wrong.

Why had I come here?

"Don't fucking patronize me; I'm going home." I felt enormously tired; alone and betrayed, which was gothic adolescent nonsense. I wasn't betrayed. Not yet.

"What did you think I could do?" Belle asked in her best psychiatrist voice, meaning *"Don't you think this is a lot of trouble to go to just to get out of a date?"*

"Tell your cop friend Hodiac that Stuart Hepburn had a motive. Ilona Saunders was his aunt, and his aunt Ilona claimed to have a family heirloom and turned up dead. Ned, who stole Books of Shadows for a hobby, stole *The Book of Moons* and wound up dead. I think that *The Book of Moons* and Ilona's heirloom are the same thing and the only person who could trace that connection is Stuart Hepburn and I'm the one with the thing now so could we please tell the police?"

"It makes more sense if Ned killed Ilona to get the book—by accident," Belle said.

"Then who killed Ned—and why?"

Ned would not kill someone for gain and then brag about his spoils later. I felt very protective of Ned, now that he was dead. He had no one else to speak for him now, to tell them that he'd meant well, or at least not as badly as things had come out. All his history and the bubble reputation that he'd sought (not in the cannon's mouth, but in living rooms like this one) were in my wardship now. There was no one else left to care.

"Bast, sometimes things just happen," Belle said helplessly. "You think that by weaving it all together into some enormous plot that only you can see, you can control it—"

"Sure. I'm sorry to take up your time." I headed for the door.

"Bast," Belle said, *"Karen."*

I stopped and looked back. Belle was invoking Karen Hightower, but she herself had helped me turn Karen into Lady Bast of the Wicca a lifetime ago. The woman she was calling—that woman's way of seeing things—no longer existed.

The lighting carved Belle's face, making her look the way she would when she was old. Once we had both believed the same things. She was the woman who had trained me. How could our internal landscapes have become so divergent?

"You don't need to mythologize your life," Belle said. "All of this criminal conspiracy—it's something you superimpose on what happens. It isn't *real.* People die. People are killed. There don't have to be reasons."

And Ned wasn't dead, nor Ilona. Possibly I didn't have an antique real-or-forged Book of Shadows on my shelf at work. I should have remembered that Belle, Lady Bellflower of the Wicca, did not believe in magic.

But she had, once. She'd told me that magic could transform the world. Which of us had changed? When had it happened?

"Stuart Hepburn had knowledge, opportunity, connection, and motive for two murders. I wish you'd find it in your heart to mention it to somebody at the police, Belle, because it's going to sound very weird coming in off the street from me. But I will."

"I think—" Belle said.

"Good night," I said. I opened the door and closed it, and as I walked down the hall I heard Belle locking up after me.

I sat in the subway heading downtown and felt cold, tired, and stupid. If Belle didn't know who I was, why did I think I was anything more than a figment of my imagination?

Too little sleep. Too little food. I'd missed dinner, and I couldn't remember having lunch, actually. I still thought I was right, but it'd been stupid to go to Belle's. What could she do?

It was weird to accuse Belle of judgmentalism, but in a way it was true. Belle wouldn't pass judgment on people, but she would judge events. And she had judged my events impossible, therefore she refused to see them.

It was, it occurred to me suddenly, the same reason Belle does not do magic, though once upon a time she'd at least talked about doing it. Magic is a part of Wicca, from the magical worldview to the spells braided into our daily lives, but Changing does no magic beyond visualization. A coven created in Belle's image.

As all covens reflect the worldview of those who form them. This was not news. And I was going to have to deal with Belle, and my anger at Belle, later. Right now I had to deal with reality. And perceptions of reality.

Cold on my bare arms. Unforgiving hard orange plastic seat sticky against the backs of my nylon-stockinged thighs. Fluorescent lighting turning my skin fish-belly white. This was reality.

Perception is a seduction. The willingness to see has to exist before anything can be seen, the encouragement of visualization that borders on the creation of phenomena without ever quite falling over the edge. To see you must be willing to see, and to place no limitations on what you may see.

The danger in that is that you may see what isn't there.

Was that how it had happened—the rift in the lute, which by and by makes the music mute? Had Belle and I, starting from the same place, both fine-tuned our perceptions of the world, hers to exclude magic, mine to include it? If two viewpoints contradict each other, mustn't one of them be right?

Or are both of them wrong?

Not in this case, I didn't think. The whole thing fitted together with a facility that was frightening. The events, at least, were real.

My mind flipped back to my first conversation with Stuart: *"I understand that the witchcult can trace its roots fairly far back,"* he'd said. He'd wanted information about Books of Shadows even then, but I'd been too blind to see it. He must have known almost nothing about *The Book of Moons* to begin with and been trying to get information at the picnic.

Had he seen Ned there—or heard him? Had he talked to Ned, somewhere in the dark hours before Ned's panic-stricken Monday call to me? Was that why Ned had left the books with me—to protect them from Stuart?

It made such a lovely plausible pattern.

Once upon a time, Ilona Saunders had a book.

Say it was an Elizabethan forgery; it could be a forgery and known to be a forgery and still be incredibly valuable if it were four centuries old. She decided to sell it to save Lothlorien . . .

*"She's bringing someone with her. Nephew. New partner in Lothlorien,"* Glitter had told me. Her only living relative, Stuart had said tonight. If you make someone your partner, sometimes you tell them where the money's coming from.

The subway rocked, accelerating on the long express run down to Fifty-ninth Street. The money. *Cherchez la gelt.* And Stuart Hepburn, child of earls, might see no reason to plow such a chunk of capital back into the marginal bookstore that was all Ilona's heart.

Argument, as inevitable as gravity. I could hear his voice in my mind: *"Oh, don't talk a lot of rot, Auntie; no one cares about a place like this anymore. But this book of yours, this book is worth millions . . ."*

Where is it?

Where is it, Auntie, dear?

Let me see it . . .

A bright Beltane morning at Lothlorien Books. Stuart Hepburn, recently from England, has arrived, at Lothlorien to escort dear Aunt Ilona to Belle's picnic. It doesn't matter why or how the topic of *The Book of Moons* comes up, or why Stuart asks to see it. By May first, Ned has already stolen it—hadn't he told me Sunday morning when we were watching Morris dancers in the park that he had a surprise announcement to make at the picnic later in the day?

She tells him about the book. Stuart asks to see

it. Is she willing? I could not imagine Ilona Saunders as anything other than forthright. She would produce it if she could.

But she couldn't.

The absence of the book must have been the cause for what came next—an accident that left Ilona dead, because why should Stuart kill her before he knew where the book was? If it was missing, they could look for it together, as allies. Or had things gone too far for that? But why kill at all when you can merely steal?

But something goes wrong and Ilona's dead. And try as he might, Stuart can't find *The Book of Moons* or a clue to its whereabouts anywhere in Lothlorien.

He could still have saved himself if he'd called the police then. Who knew?—if he'd called an ambulance immediately, Ilona Saunders might be alive today.

But he doesn't. Stuart Hepburn, murderer, leaves Ilona dead and goes looking for an alibi, for information—maybe even looking for Ned. Ned was Ilona's clerk. He was the next likely person to question.

And there was one thing I would bank on, the more I thought it over: Stuart *did* get to the picnic in time to hear Ned announce to everybody in earshot that he, Ned Skelton, had the grimore of Mary, Queen of Scots—Ilona's *Book of Moons.*

Did he mark Ned down for death then? Or was it later? Was he the burglar of Ned's apartment as well as the murderer? And why did Stuart kill *again* without proof that the book that was his ostensible goal could be gained by his actions?

I'd never know. But there was one thing I knew now: Stuart Hepburn did not act in good faith, not from the first moment I saw him. He mingled at the picnic, pumping all of us for information we didn't know we were giving. Looking for Ilona's book, for information about Ilona's book, for places such books could be found.

Maybe even trying to find out how seriously we Witches took Ned's claim, and if we would pay money for Ilona's treasure.

*And presented himself as a seeker, without any of the round-eyed wonder exhibited by new seekers who find the Craft. Stuart was determined to be unflappable, no matter how strange we were, because he wanted in . . .*

*That* was the not-quite-rightness that had bothered me about him from the first. We are not mainstream, we of the Community, and you either love our weirdness or hate it. You do not ignore it as if it does not exist, not unless the stakes are very high indeed.

It took Stuart until Monday night to find out where Ned lived, or else to catch Ned's apartment empty. Assuming he was the burglar, he broke in looking for the book—only the book wasn't there either. I already had it. He came up dry.

So then he had to talk to Ned Tuesday night. Ned was frightened on Monday when he found out about Ilona, but he wasn't on Tuesday when he asked me to bless his apartment. Had he talked to Stuart in the meantime? Did Stuart convince him that he had nothing to fear? Stuart could be plausible; I was living proof of that.

So Stuart came to see Ned Tuesday night. And kill Ned Tuesday night. Frustration, or fear, or just covering his tracks; had Ned taunted him with the fact that *The Book of Moons* was beyond Stuart's reach?

But Stuart, for whatever reason, killed Ned without either getting what he had come for or even finding out where it was. And I was pretty sure that was what had happened, because that same night Weiser's, the Snake, and Mirror Mirror were broken into by someone who cleaned out their weird rare book sections.

Stuart.

Looking for *The Book of Moons* in the only other place he could think of. Finding nothing.

And then—and this new intuition made me slightly ill—coming back to his one inside informant on the witchcraft scene. Me. To dine and dazzle, looking for new leads.

Was the killer really Stuart? Who else could it be? There were too many indicators pointing in his direction.

Granted, Ilona's death could be the result of a random robbery that went wrong. But Ned was—what was Glitter's word for it?—professionally "whacked" within a ninety-minute early-evening window a full twenty-four hours after his apartment had been burgled.

Call that coincidence, too, if you're Belle. But answer a few questions first.

What was Ned's motive for leaving the package filled with Books of Shadows with me? For safekeeping? Why didn't he think his apartment was safe? How did he decide it wasn't safe *before* it was burgled? Did he know someone was going to break in?

And if he left the Books of Shadows with me so that I could return them, why include *The Book of*

*Moons*, when he knew Ilona was dead? Who was I supposed to return it to? I certainly couldn't return it to the woman who had written it. Who was alleged to have written it. To Mary, doomed, manipulated Mary, thrown out of her French coven to die in a foreign homeland she could not remake in her own image.

And, if not Stuart Hepburn, then who found it necessary, the same night Ned was murdered to break into not one, but *three* occult bookstores? Had Ned told Stuart the book was in a safe place? Had Stuart killed him before finding out anything more?

I thought of the book and its hunters: a mad, Maltese Falcon chase down through the centuries. And now the *La Paloma* had docked and I was the new stalking horse, just as soon as *The Book of Moons* could be tracked to me.

I sat on the subway feeling spooked, but that was stupid. Knowing about Stuart did not change my life at all. We all live in cities full of murderers every day. It's just that we never look into their faces.

# 8

I felt like mugging bait walking home from the subway stop. I wondered if there actually was something to Lace's "clothing as victimization" rap. Either way, I thought I was going to give this damn dress and all its accessories to The Cat.

It was a little after midnight. Since noon I'd had two ounces of Scotch and a lot of adrenaline. If there was anything compromised about my locks it didn't register. I walked inside and closed the door.

Stuart Hepburn was waiting for me inside my apartment.

Realization came in a jerky series of epiphanies. The dishevelment of the space where I lived. The books on the floor. The curls of brown paper where he'd unwrapped the two books I'd brought back here. The bathroom light on, but the main room light out so I'd come all the way in.

And Stuart sitting on my bed.

*Oh, yes, of course,* was my first thought, tainted by faint self-reproach: after four burglaries and two murders, would the Stuart of my creation have stopped there?

"My door looked fine," I said. It was an effort to talk; my tongue felt thick and unresponsive, as if I were drunk.

"Occasionally I can be subtle. Where is it? It wasn't at that pesthole where you work."

There was only one "it."

"I don't have it," I suggested. I'd left it at the studio when I'd gone out with all the other books. Why hadn't he found it there?

Stuart smiled. He was still dressed as he had been earlier in the evening, in the expensive, understated dark suit.

"If you don't have it, I'll kill you," he said, smiling, and I knew it for the simple truth. "You have it or you know where it is. The card you left with poor Neddie was enough reason to search your office, but when I didn't find it there, I wasn't sure about you. Until dinner. Why else would you have run out on me except to make sure it was still safe?"

The truth, they say, will set you free.

"Because I knew you'd killed Ilona—"

"Oh, don't give me any of that witchy claptrap," Stuart interrupted scornfully. "If you had any supernatural powers you'd hardly be here now, would you?"

He had a certain point. I wished I weren't here now. But I simply hadn't been paying attention, in a city where inattention is fatal.

Stuart got up and walked toward me, and only then did I realize that the shock and fright had kept me standing there when I might have run. He took out a tiny gun, silver and pearl-handled, barely as big as his hand but big enough to kill. A .22 or .25; I knew this from a book on self-defense the studio did once.

I wondered if it was the same one he'd used on Ned and felt a wave of nausea fill my mouth with thick saliva. Stuart came and stood in front of me, pointing the gun.

"Ned had your card, darling, and for the longest time I couldn't figure out why—but you Witches stick together, don't you?"

It was so far from true that it was funny. I shook my head. Stuart thought I was arguing with him. Everything I said seemed to make him angry and I didn't know how to stop that.

"You have the book. Ned gave it to you. He didn't have it when we had our little chat, but he did have your card, right there by the phone. Who would he give it to, but you?"

Stuart's faith in me was nearly flattering.

"It's not here," I repeated, docile and truthful as a small child.

"I know that," said Stuart. "I've already looked. You're going to take me to it—I won't make the same mistake twice."

The little gun glittered in the overhead light. There was nothing I could do now. Magic could keep me from meeting the gunman. It could keep the gun from being drawn. But this was the real world, and no spell would stop a bullet.

"You thought you knew where it was before," I said, reasoning it out as if the right answers would save me. "That's why you killed Ned. You thought you had it, but you didn't."

"Bright girl," Stuart said approvingly. I shivered

as if someone was pouring alcohol on my skin and might any moment set it alight.

"The book is mine," Stuart said. "I want it back. That's all. Stealing is a sin, you know."

I wondered what Stuart's views were on murder.

My mind seemed to be racing, as if I had to do all the thinking for the rest of my life in the next few minutes. I thought about the fact that death is silence and the involuntary archaic smile, that people killing or thinking about killing do not exhibit Stuart's drawing-room glibness. I understood the reason why in an instant: Stuart was hiding past and future murders from himself and pretending this was common social bullying. Plus gun.

I felt a desperate need to help him, to make polite conversation and conceal horror beneath a shield of metaphor and analogy.

"Where is the book?" Stuart said with surprising patience, and the millrace of discourse opened again in my mind: he said he'd searched the studio and he hadn't found it. But the studio was where I'd left it, and if he already knew it wasn't here, what could I tell him that he'd believe when the truth wouldn't help me?

I shook my head.

"I am waiting," Stuart said. "Where is the book now?"

My skin was dry ice, gathering moisture from the air. My eyes burned as sweat trickled down my face, down my skin under the dress.

The book. Mary's *Book of Moons*. The Craft must ever survive; this is built into our mythology—the Burning Times; six centuries when our struggle was not to stay alive, but to pass our tradition beyond our deaths.

As this shadow-Mary, wavering indistinct between history and fabulation, had. Her book had survived her beheading, taken and hidden by conspirators loyal, if not to her, then to their Goddess. Taken and hidden. And hidden, hidden, hidden . . .

"Of course it's at the studio," I said coolly, as if I could buy into Stuart's sociable lie. "Did you look inside the stat camera?"

"You're bluffing. Why would you hide it? You couldn't know I'd be looking for it," Stuart said. The gun gestured: flick away. Flick back.

"Witches hide their books, Stuart, from *cowans* like you."

Like so many of our words, *cowan* is Scots, and, as we use it, simply means "non-Witch." Stuart, however, seemed to be impressed with being a *cowan,* because he relaxed just a little.

"All right, Witchie-poo. Let's go back to the studio—and you can show me where it is."

I felt the immanence of violence retreat, enough to allow me anger.

"Afraid you'll shoot someone else too soon?" I said.

And Stuart hit me.

It was stunning; unexpected as a flash of lightning. It knocked me off those silly treacherous heels I was wearing. I fell to the floor, sliding on the linoleum. One of my big crescent moon earrings, torn off by the blow, slid across the floor and under the sink. I could hear the sound it made clearly. Then the pain rolled in, slow and heavy as thunder, while I lay on the floor in complete incomprehension of what had just happened to me.

"Get up," said Stuart, and understanding came. He'd hit me, maybe with the gun. I shook my head. Bright heat lightning danced over the surface of the pain-thunder, making me catch my breath in a jerky stutter. Blood eddied through my saliva, but there was no blood on the floor, only the cuts on the inside of my mouth that my teeth had made.

"Get up," Stuart said again.

I kicked my shoes the rest of the way off and got to my hands and knees. His shoes were very close to my face. I thought for a moment that he would kick me, and there was nothing I could do to stop him.

But he didn't. The relief made me almost grateful to him.

I got up and sat quickly down on my kitchen chair, shaking like an addict. I touched my face. It was hot and tender. My lip left smears of lipstick and blood on my fingers. Automatically I took out the remaining crescent earring. I could not look at Stuart.

"I like a girl who knows how to behave herself," Stuart said affably. I didn't say anything. I'd learned better.

"Come on, Witchie. Upsie-daisy. That's a good girl," Stuart said.

My boots were under the kitchen table where I'd left them last. I bent forward carefully and pulled them toward me. In nylon stockings my feet slid into them easily.

"Very nice," Stuart said. He was relishing this as if in retaliation for a lifetime's humiliation, but I could not imagine what I could have done to him that required this scale of vengeance. More than abandoning him during a date, surely? Who was I standing in for, in Stuart's mental landscape?

I got the boots on and stood up. The side of my face that he'd hit felt sunburned, and the ear was beginning to sting. My mind was rehearsing the possibility of future pain.

At the door I got my jacket, because shock, the body's instinctive response to threat, was freezing me to death.

I took the wad of keys off the shelf beside the door and stuck them in the jacket pocket. I picked up my hat and put that on, too, trying to convince some part of myself that everything was all right. Then I stepped out into the hall and Stuart followed me.

Stuart put the gun away, but not far away. He didn't let me lock the door when we left. It was foolish of him to give me such proof when I could still withhold what he wanted. But it was proof I didn't need. I already knew that, as far as Stuart was concerned, I would never come back here again.

The subway doesn't go there, Stuart had no car, and there were no taxis anywhere at this hour of the morning. We walked to Houston Graphics. Stuart held me by the scruff of my jacket and twisted it every time I moved my arms. The gun was in his pocket, handy to hand. This was New York. He could shoot me on this midnight street in perfect safety. No one would come if they heard a gunshot. No one would come if I screamed. No one would even call the police.

Life was composed of odd disjointed sensations. The wind, cold and fresh in the early morning. Distant sirens. Indignation, that I wasn't dressed right for a crisis. The pain in my face as I licked my bleeding lip. The knowledge that my boots were rubbing a blister into my right heel. Grateful relief, because now Stuart was behaving candidly—no more acts, no more deception.

As we walked he chatted companionably, as if he were not suspended between killings over the abyss in which lives the knowledge that there is no more external reason either to act or to refrain. I forgot each word as he spoke it. Incipient mortality scoured me into a desolation beyond ego.

We arrived.

Houston Graphics is not located in a neighborhood I would choose to frequent at this hour—as individual neighborhoods have gotten glossier, the whole fabric of New York life has rotted as if there were some metaphysical constant of niceness, and the concentration of it in some places has left others vulnerable to some existential plague.

There was traffic on Broadway, even now. While we waited for the light, a gust down the concrete canyon whisked my hat off. I grabbed for it reflexively, but Stuart yanked me off balance and I watched it vanish under the wheels of a cab.

"You won't be needing that, pet," Stuart said. My hat made a popping sound as it was flattened: echo of a gunshot.

Stuart hummed to himself. We crossed like law-abiding out-of-towners and Stuart led me to the doorway of Houston's building.

Where the door was covered with a steel shutter that I did not have the keys to open.

There was no way for Stuart to prove or disprove my story tonight. I felt a giddy wash of relief.

I was feeling safe when Stuart's hidden hand came out of the pocket with a wad of keys. He shoved them at me.

"One of these should fit. Don't gawp at me, poppet—our Neddie's been far more useful in death than he ever was in life."

I looked down at what I held in my hand—Ned Skelton's ring of master keys. Stuart's entrée to my apartment—and to Houston Graphics, earlier this evening.

I felt a dangerous and proprietary anger fill me, as if Ned were still alive to be hurt. But I held it down, concentrating on finding the key that would bypass the padlock, just as the padlock on the Snake's outer shutters had been bypassed Tuesday night.

The fifth one fit. I unlocked the padlock and loosened the chain and ran the steel shutter up, baring the door. Maybe its being open at this hour would look odd enough to stop a prowl car, but Stuart wasn't from New York; it didn't bother him.

I used my own keys for the rest. I thought I'd have trouble with the locks, but my hands had trembled far worse for much less than my approaching death. I opened the street door (two keys), then the lobby inner door that's supposed to be a security measure (one key). They're both glass. The outer door has a spring lock and dead bolt. It snapped shut behind me, but the crash bar would open it from the inside.

Of course, none of these measures would have been in place earlier this evening when Stuart had searched Houston Graphics. He'd done it while I was waiting for him at Top of the Sixes—that was the only time he could be sure I wouldn't be there. Ned's keys had gotten him into the studio, and I hoped for the sake of my fellow employees that no one had been there, because Stuart Hepburn seemed to think casual murder the ideal solution for Life's petty annoyances.

I wondered if the police had been to see him at all, or if that tale was just the one pointless lie that had unraveled Stuart so that I could see what he had done.

I think I had a plan.

The lobby was dim. I didn't bother to light it—that was a danger signal even an out-of-towner would pick up on, though in a few hours the building would be lit anyway, open for business.

A few hours. Such a short time when you're sleeping. Such a long time, when someone's pointing a gun at you.

We crossed the lobby. The elevator was probably locked down for the night, and habit made me choose the stairs anyway. Every step jarred my bruised jaw. Stuart, following me up, kept his gun pointed at my kidneys.

Houston shares the building's third floor with a theatrical costumer and a low-end typesetter. The door has a key lock, a snap-bolt, and a key-turn dead bolt, none of which will lock by themselves. I opened the door's three locks and stepped inside.

"Where's this stat camera?" Stuart said.

On some level I'd managed to forget he was with me. I jumped when he spoke and dropped both sets of keys. He smiled and followed me in, shutting the door behind him. Neither of us locked the door or picked up the keys.

"Over there," I said. My voice was parched and tiny. I flipped on the overhead lights.

And then I turned around and looked, really looked, at what Stuart had done to the studio.

I groaned. Stuart chuckled, pleased. He took the gun out and waved it. Firearms, the chic urban accessory.

No one could have been here when he'd come. I imagined him, in his expensive, impeccable suit, ripping through everything like a spoiled child who would never be called to account for his actions.

Mikey Pontifex's desk rose up out of a nest of trashed paperwork: letters, memos, files. Its drawers hung open like the tongues of exhaustion. Ray's worktable was similarly trashed; boards and veluxes and transparencies blown up in a willful hurricane and all the billing hopelessly pied.

The bookshelves that line two walls of the studio were mostly empty, their books thrown on the floor, and around the white-painted corners of the carrels I could see a pale tide of jumbled ruined paper where Stuart had dumped the contents of everyone's storage shelves on the floor.

"Come *on*, Witchie." Stuart jabbed me in the back with the gun again. "I'd hate to think you were having me on."

*What would you do if I were?* I didn't say, and tried to stifle my own speculation about the answer. After two murders and two failures, I was pretty sure that Stuart was not going to shoot me until he was actually holding *The Book of Moons* in his hands. But

there were so many other things he could do short of
that.

"It's in the stat camera," I said. "Inside."

But it wasn't. I'd left it safely wrapped and labeled
and in plain sight, as far as I could remember, and if
Stuart hadn't found it, where was it?

I couldn't look for it now.

"Well, go on," Stuart said.

I walked over to the corner of the room where the
big blue monster crouched. The stat camera is a re-
ducer/enlarger, a camera, and developer all in one.
It's eight feet long and four feet high and about three
feet across. You put your original on the gray sponge
mat with the white registration lines screened onto it
and lock the glass plate over it to hold it still. Then
you rotate the bed into an upright position and go
back to the other end of the machine to make your
stat.

You set the exposure time (by guess and experience and—as a last resort—by the manual) and you
set the percentage of original size, from 25 to 250
percent, based on what you've run up on your scal-
ing ruler.

The paper's loaded in twenty-five-foot rolls in a
cassette that's kept inside the machine. You cut it to
size by touch, with your hands stuck through rubber
cuffs that keep the inside of the machine light-safe,
and position it on the glass, and lock it down. When
you press the button, there's a sound like main
phasers firing, and the blinding light of the stat
lamps. In the absence of paper, when the light is on
you can stare down at a ghost image reflected onto
the glass. It's helpful for positioning the photographic paper, but after a while you don't bother. At

last—carefully, by touch, in the dark—you feed your exposed paper into the endlessly turning rollers and hope that *la machine* will send it through its various chemical baths and rinse and leave you, in the end, with a black-and-white photostat that you can use.

Every Tuesday morning Royce takes the cover off, mixes new developer, changes the chemicals, makes sure the belts are aligned, and removes tiny shreds of paper from the gears. The job takes about four hours.

I walked over to the sink behind the camera and splashed water on my face. My face in the little mirror above the sink was red-eyed and set, unappealingly terrified, but serenity was settling over me with soft implacable weight. It would be so easy to let go of this world and robe myself in the *ekstasis* that made Indian warriors certain that painted shirts would stop bullets.

And then—without fear, without judgment—I would turn to Stuart and demand that he give me the gun.

No. Not now.

And a small inner voice answered: *not yet.*

I sorted through the wreckage at Royce's station until I found the stat machine's tool kit. The phone was here too, for some reason, sitting placidly on Royce's stool as if divorcing itself from the chaos below.

"What are you dawdling for?" Stuart said. He was standing by the door, waving the gun. It had a good chance of being inaccurate at this distance, not that that was any inducement to rebellion.

"Do you expect me to open it with my fingernails?" I snapped, brave because he was standing so far away. But he was standing between me and the door and I already knew he was stronger than I was.

The phone rang.

*Here. Go,* the inner voice said.

I lost all fear. I lost all sense of threat. I scooped it up and answered it—not for defiance, and certainly not because I thought the caller could help me—it was almost certainly, at this hour, a wrong number. But habit is that which is drilled into the nerves, beyond the grip of the mind. The phone rang, so I answered it.

"Bookie-Joint-Can-I-Help-You?" my voice sang out, assured and serene.

Stuart frowned, and shifted his weight forward, and raised the gun. I smiled brightly at him, having gone past the place where fear was.

"This is Sam. Is Karen there?" A male voice. A nice one, but worried.

"No," I said cheerfully, "she isn't here, can I take a message? Do you know what time it is?" I added, for verisimilitude's sake.

The clock on the wall said 2:00 A.M. There was a long crack down its glass that I didn't remember ever seeing before.

"Can you talk freely?" the voice asked cautiously. Stuart made "hang-up" motions at me as I smiled gaily at him. There was only the one phone; Stuart had no way of listening to what Sam-my-late-night-caller said.

"No, of course not," I said. "What kind of a moron are you? I don't know when your job will be ready. Don't call back."

"I understand," the voice said. Calm, alert, unknown.

Stuart charged for me. I put the phone back in the cradle.

"Who was that?" Stuart demanded, grabbing the phone away from me. His face was white and stretched, as masklike as mine had looked in the mirror.

The bright hysteric defiance collapsed. I bent forward as the world grayed out and left me shaking, weak, and nauseated. My mouth was dry and tasted foul. Magic—any extraordinary effort—takes its toll.

Stuart threw the phone across the room. It whipped to the end of its tether and landed with a jangle. The dial tone began to drone, loud in the early A.M. stillness. Stuart ran over to it and kicked it into silence. I could hear his breathing from where I was, and the sound finished anchoring me to my body and the world.

"Don't you do that again! Don't you ever do that again!" Stuart shouted, white-faced with fury. My eyes were drawn to the silvery flicker of the gun barrel, as if it were the most important thing in the room.

It occurred to me, distantly, that I was banking far too much on Stuart's reasonable self-interest. After two murders and several dead ends his grip on plausible normalcy was rapidly eroding, and unlike Witches and magicians, who cross the unmarked mental borders leading to the psychic shadowland frequently, Stuart did not have a way back into the territory of his daylight mind. The strongest social taboo had been broken: he had killed, and now he might do anything.

I saw him drowning in that knowledge, and realized that he could shoot me at any time, for any reason.

Or for no reason at all.

*"Who was it?"* Stuart shouted.

"Someone for Royce," I said, and closed my eyes. I felt tears in the back of my voice and the serpent-terror that could get me killed by making me too reckless to live.

"Get to work," Stuart said. He rubbed the barrel of the gun against his jaw, then seemed to remember what he held and where it should be pointing. A smile appeared intermittently on his face; utterly meaningless. He no longer looked at all human.

I felt a megalomaniac certainty that I could handle this situation and I knew that I was wrong. I could wait, I could play for time, and when there was no more time I could wrap myself in the Goddess's light and let Her choose for me. That was all.

Carefully, as if Stuart's attention were a bomb I did not wish to trigger, I took off my jacket and put it on Royce's stool.

"I'm going to use the screwdriver to take off the cowling," I said aloud, as if I were defusing a bomb and every word was being recorded. To speak at all was an effort.

Stuart made another meaningless smile. I hoped he wouldn't shoot me when he saw the screwdriver in my hand, but after this long, it was getting hard to care.

Sweat poured off me as if I were desperately ill. I could smell myself; acrid and metallic. Fear sweat is different from any other kind.

I began hunting for the screws. I had to find them quickly. I was supposed to have done this before. I'd seen Royce do it lots and lots. If Stuart got tired of watching me do this he'd shoot me, and even though the stopping power of a .22 or .25 is minimal at anything other than extreme close range, I did not want Stuart to shoot me.

Not because I thought he'd kill me. But because I thought that once he fired the gun he would finally snap, and I did not want to be here when he did.

The amnesia of shock made me alternately forget my caller named Sam and obsess on him. I found myself believing that he would come and rescue me, and realized that hope was just another form of the terror that holds you still until you can be killed. He might be help, but I did not dare bet my life on it.

And I had a plan.

Without a plan I could not have built the fantasy of control that let me act in a way that would keep me alive. I actually managed to worry about what was happening to my unlocked apartment because I had a plan.

I had a weapon that Stuart didn't know about.

The photographic process requires two stages: the developer to bring the latent image out on the paper, and the fixer to halt the process before the paper turns completely black. The fixer, though I wouldn't want to get it into my eyes, is a fairly mild chemical, but the developer is caustic. Once I got the camera disassembled, I'd have a bath of dilute acid in my hands.

I was going to throw it at Stuart and run. The door wasn't locked. Small handguns are supposed to be untrustworthy. I'd take my chances on the street.

If I could.

I found the screws and unthreaded them. There

were eight. I pulled them out and set them aside. They rolled downhill, away from the machine. I lifted the cowling off the back half of the machine. It made hollow booming noises as it was shifted.

"Where is it?" Stuart said, shoving me aside. The cowling shifted in my fingers and cut them; it was thin metal. I set it down quickly. He stared down at what looked like a miniature printing press.

"I don't see it; if you're lying to me, you bitch, I'll—"

"It's in the camera," I said. "Underneath." Exhaustion helped make my voice flat and ultimately believable. Stuart backed off, waving his little chrome pistol.

"Hurry up," he said.

"If I hurry too much the book'll get wet. If that happens, it's ruined."

I don't know where this fund of plausible invention came from; I spend so much time learning to tell the truth that lying doesn't come very easily. But it was there when I needed it; the gift of the Goddess.

Stuart backed off.

And perhaps it was Her will as well that Stuart should take such an implausible story as mine seriously. But the Moon is the mistress of illusion; the Elizabethans believed Her light could drive men mad.

If I were Royce and this were any Tuesday morning, the next thing would be to lift out and clean the rollers, exposing the chemical baths. But if I did that, Stuart would see there was no place in the machine for a book to be hidden. Right now he was watching me closely; I'd never get the moment's grace I needed to work my plan while he was doing that.

I was calm, wonderfully so. But I didn't seem to be able to think very well. And if I stood here much longer trying to decide what to do, Stuart would get suspicious. I started removing the cowling from the front half of the machine.

Stuart retreated to the other side of the room.

I'd never seen this part done. It probably hadn't been done since the thing was assembled at the factory; it was no part of the maintenance routine, but Stuart didn't know that. The screws were frozen solid, and my fingers were slippery with blood and sweat. I finally had to wrap paper towels around my hands to get a grip on the screwdriver.

When I started to lift the cowling loose I realized there was something still holding it in place. I pulled anyway, and felt something catch, resist, tear, and finally give.

The sound of a footstep was loud in the room.

I jerked toward Stuart, but he hadn't moved. He was on the other side of the studio, staring at the clock and half sitting on Mikey's desk, jogging his foot in the air as if he were waiting impatiently. The gun was resting on his knee, almost harmless.

He hadn't heard the sound; neither had he made it.

The sound came again. Someone walking, but if I'd heard it, Stuart had to have, and he never moved.

*There was someone else in the building, moving quietly. Moving toward me.*

I looked at the clock. It seemed as if hours had passed, but it was only two-thirty. Half an hour since we'd gotten here.

Half an hour since the phone rang.

The stat camera is set along the short end of the

rectangular bite out of the Houston Graphics studio space, which means that when you're standing near the sink at the head of the stat camera you're at the one place in the studio that isn't in sight of the door.

I set the cowling down and went back to the head of the camera. Stuart looked up, but I made sure I wasn't looking toward him when he did.

I began lifting the rollers out. They're almost three feet long and heavy; their weight is what holds the trays of fixer and developer steady. If I were a comic book hero I would have tried to bludgeon Stuart with one, but, choreography aside, I'm not certain that I could have managed to hit him with the force required to do any more than make him mad.

I lifted the rinse tray out and balanced it on the side of the machine.

Someone coming closer; a palpable certainty that raised the hair on my arms. Stuart noticed it at last, or noticed something. He got to his feet and started toward me. I lifted the developer bath in my hands.

The door of the studio hit the wall with the sound of an explosion.

"Hold it!" someone shouted.

I threw myself flat, sliding in a puddle of chemicals. The machine blocked my view. My eyes watered with the fumes of spilled developer. I saw nothing. There were no loud sounds, only breathing and the scuff of shoes and some faint jingling sounds, and, after a moment, Stuart's voice, small and irritable:

"I didn't do anything!"

# 9

It was a quarter of three Thursday morning, and things were different. Sam's last name was Hodiac. He was round, chocolate brown, and balding; dark-skinned and ten years and change older than I was. There was a gold shield hung on a chain around his neck and a gun on his belt and he looked open and friendly and reassuring, except for the eyes.

They were cop eyes, as giving as glass. That, too, was reassurance of a sort.

He was Belle's cop, and he was here.

"When Izzy mentioned Mr. Hepburn, you better believe I got moving," he said to me. "It's a good thing for you that I did. But we've had our eye on Mr. Hepburn for awhile now," he added.

Izzy is Isobel. Belleflower. Who had, despite all our differences, made the phone call that had saved my life. If she'd waited until morning it would have been too late, unless my plan had worked.

I thought of telling Lieutenant Hodiac about my plan and decided he wouldn't appreciate it.

I was sitting in Mikey's chair behind Mikey's desk

at the studio. We were in the midst of a full-blown crime scene, and no one had let me make coffee, a fact that grated irrationally on my nerves. We had Lieutenant Hodiac and two uniformed patrolmen and another detective whose case this actually was. There'd actually been four uniformed officers until two of them had taken Stuart away in handcuffs and Stuart's gun away in a little plastic bag.

Stuart maintained that he hadn't done anything.

"Stuart Hepburn killed Ilona Saunders and Ned Skelton," I said. I'd probably said it before. It was, I'd found, an opinion also held by our friends the police—who, until *The Book of Moons* was added to the equation, could not understand why Stuart would wish to do this.

"That shooter of his is going to tell us most of what we need to know," Hodiac said. He sounded pleased.

"Oh, good," I said inadequately. I felt numb, as if crying would be appropriate if only I could work up the interest.

A patrolman came in and handed something to Hodiac, who wrung it in his hands and then handed it to me. It was one of those cold bags that freeze when you twist them. I held it to my jaw, wishing everyone would leave me alone.

"Are you all right? Do you want someone to take you to the hospital?" Hodiac asked.

"I'm fine." I don't have insurance. "Thank you for coming," I added, feeling I had to say something.

Hodiac smiled. "It's our job, miss."

One of the patrolmen came back with coffees from the deli next door. Hodiac sorted through them and handed one to me. After what Stuart had done to the studio, our coffeemaker was probably broken anyway.

"Drink it, miss. It'll help."

"Bast," I said. "It's Bast."

Not Karen. Not "miss". Not "Witchie" or "sweetheart" or "pet." My name is Bast.

I sipped it. It was tepid and horribly sweet. I shivered.

"It isn't going to work out quite the way you see in the movies, but I think we'll be able to hold on to Mr. Hepburn," Hodiac said. "You may not have to testify in court." This was supposed to be reassuring. "Detective Larsen will explain the procedure to you, and what you need to do. Here's my card. You can call me if you need anything."

I looked for a pocket to put it in and realized I didn't have my jacket. I set the card on the desk, lining it up carefully with the edge. Lieutenant Hodiac was called away. I finished the coffee, winced at the sugar pooled in the bottom, and walked over to where my jacket was.

"It's mine," I said to the officer who'd followed me. He looked a young fifteen, if that, and had a white-on-black tag on his shirt that said his name was Sanchez.

I put on my jacket. It didn't make me feel any warmer. I realized the entire front of my little black dress was soaking wet and my nylons were nothing but snags. My boots were wet. Every muscle, without exception, hurt.

"Detective Larsen wonders if you could talk to him now, miss," Officer Sanchez said politely.

I wondered what he'd do if I said no. I was tired beyond imagining; I would gladly tell them anything in the world if they'd just let me sleep.

*I slept not since the Conquest / Nor since then have I waked—*

Mad Tom. Bedlam's boys are bonnie. I wondered if girls were allowed into their club. I wondered where you went to sign up. I walked back over to the desk.

Detective Larsen was an unshaven blond wearing a pale blue sport jacket over jeans and the gold shield medallion *du jour.* He was probably singing arias of thanksgiving at the prospect of being able to clear two murders off his caseload. I sat down. I smiled. He smiled. Meaningless.

He took particulars: name, address, phone number, profession. Had I really been working here this long? I wondered. Then we got down to specifics.

Detective Larsen interrupted me every other sentence with questions until I got the idea of what he wanted to hear. Had Stuart shown me the gun? Yes. Had he threatened me verbally? Yes—he'd said he'd kill me. Had he threatened me physically in any way? He'd hit me.

Detective Larsen seemed pleased that Stuart had hit me. I was glad somebody was pleased. We went on.

Stuart had broken into my apartment using passkeys stolen from his previous victim Ned Skelton. Stuart brought me to the studio at gunpoint, because I had told him that the rare book that Ned Skelton had stolen from Ned's employer—Stuart's aunt—and stashed with me, was here. No, I hadn't known what it was when Ned had left it with me; I'd found out later. No, I hadn't thought it was odd that he'd do that. Well, yes and no. Okay, never mind.

I'd been supposed to meet Ned the night he was murdered—

"Why?" Detective Larsen said.

"I was going to do a blessing on his apartment."

"Why's that?" Larsen said sharply.

Hodiac had come over to listen. I stared supplicatingly at him, feeling the fear that all of us fringefolk feel when our explanations may be twisted into unintended confessions.

"She's a Wiccan, Don," Hodiac said. "She blesses people."

"Oh," Larsen said, losing interest in that line of inquiry. "One of them. Go on, miss."

I went back to Tuesday night. I'd seen the police take Ned's body out of his apartment. We went over the time that Ned had called me and the time I got there, including why I thought those times were right and then (in my statement) I came back to the studio. I opened the box and found the book, and thought that Ned must have taken it from Ilona.

"Why'd you think that?" Larsen said.

Because it had been in a box with all the other Books of Shadows that Ned had stolen and Ilona's was the only place it could have come from, but if I told him that, what would he do?

"I don't know," I said unconvincingly. I rubbed the bridge of my nose. "Ilona was related to Mary, Queen of Scots," I said, and at the time it sounded like a reasonable explanation.

Hodiac said something to Larsen that I didn't hear.

"We can come back to that. What did you do then?" Larsen said to me.

I'd done nothing, wondering what to do with the book since Ilona and Ned were both dead. And Wednesday night, Stuart had been waiting in my apartment.

Reality, as simplified for the legal process.

While we'd been talking, phone calls had been made from the Rolodex—though not from the studio phone—once the police'd found it. Mikey and Ray would arrive as soon as they could make it from Fort Lee and Fort Hamilton Parkway, respectively.

Larsen walked off. Hodiac knelt by the chair, bringing himself down to eye level with me.

"Don's okay," Hodiac said. "He just wants to get everything straight for the charge sheet. You'll need to come down to the precinct to make your statement and so on; probably talk to the DA. I'm afraid it's going to take a while, but we'll try to make it as quick as we can. Are you ready to go? Sanchez can take you down. Don has a few things to finish up here."

"My apartment's unlocked." I guess I realized then I was going to live, and, living, had to take up my responsibilities again.

"I can have Sanchez take you by there on the way downtown. He can go up with you, check out your apartment, make sure everything's all right."

"Oh, good," I said.

"Why didn't Hepburn find this *Book of Moons* he was looking for?" Hodiac said. "Didn't you leave it here?"

"It was supposed to be here," I said. "But it wasn't here, and I don't know where it is," I said, and finally started to cry.

* * *

Mikey got to the studio a few minutes later. I was still there. Mikey Pontifex has tiny brown eyes and thin greige hair and stands five-foot-four in his socks. He looked at the wreckage of the studio, the cops, the remains of his stat camera. His face turned redder and redder and then he noticed me.

"You'd better have a good explanation for this," Mikey said to me.

I didn't. But I did have some advice that I earnestly encouraged him to take. Officer Sanchez put his hand gently on my arm and pulled, gently. I walked out with him. The hall was decked with yellow tape. POLICE LINE: DO NOT CROSS. We crossed it.

Where is the boundary between the real and the unreal? Between faith and insanity? Between the world of the Gods and the pleasant realms of Men?

I met Ray on the stairs.

"Jesus Christ, what happened to your face?" Ray demanded.

"Another beautiful day in Paradise," I said. He went up. Sanchez and I went down.

The material world was the flat fake dark that it only gets between well after midnight and just before dawn. I rode in the back of what Officer Sanchez called his unit and gave directions to my apartment.

When we got there, he got out of the car and came around to let me out. There are no door handles in the backseats of police cars.

We went upstairs. He called me ma'am and suggested I let him go first. His belt was covered with loops and pouches and boxes in black leather with nickel-plated snaps. He carried a revolver and a nightstick and a walkie-talkie as long as my forearm that murmured constantly to itself in *gematria* and static, but I wasn't afraid of him. He was safe.

I was safe.

No one had been in my apartment. Officer Sanchez pushed the door open very carefully and shined his light all around before he flipped the switch, but the place looked just the way Stuart and I had left it. Officer Sanchez looked in my bathroom. He looked in my closet. Nothing was gone. No one was there. No one had noticed this vulnerability.

I wondered if this was all that strength was: a vulnerability unnoticed through the exercise of random chance. Maybe nobody's strong, only lucky.

Officer Sanchez inspected my door. He told me that my locks were all still functional, but that I might like to get them replaced anyway; a secular charm against invasion.

He made me feel middle-aged and unworldly, and though I was happy to have him there I resented the fact that what had torn my life so far apart didn't seem to touch him at all.

I wanted to change clothes but he said not to. I compromised, grabbing socks for the boots, a warmer coat. My hands were shaking. Officer Sanchez locked my door for me and then handed me my keys. I clutched them so hard it hurt—distantly, as though the person being hurt were someone else.

We went back out into the night.

It was eight o'clock in the morning before I got back from what its inhabitants refer to—with varying degrees of facetiousness—as the Palace. One Police Plaza.

I had had bad coffee and vending-machine food. I had told my story to several detectives several times, and finally to someone from the DA's office; flurries of activity interspersed with hours of waiting while people waited for other people to show up. I carefully answered only the questions I was asked, and it turned out they didn't care a lot about Ned's package or my intuitions; they expected to match Stuart's gun to the bullet that killed Ned, and in the fashion of law as distinct from justice, were not going to bother with anything but their single strongest case.

The machine of bureaucracy, as adapted to enforcement. They took pictures of my bruises. I didn't see Stuart. They were careful about that. It was kindness.

I refused lawyers and EMTs and finally got to sign my statement. There was a grand jury appearance in the not-so-distant future, where the People of the State of New York would decide if what Stuart had done would merit a trial. It was a formality, Detective Larsen assured me. I might even not be called. They hadn't decided yet. There would definitely be a trial.

A marked car drove me home, clutching business cards and form-subpoenas and a list of instructions. The daylight and color seemed wrong and unreal; a world of life and reason that I shouldn't be able to see, somehow.

The door was still locked. I unlocked it, went inside, locked it again.

I took off my coat and hung it up carefully. I took off my boots and put them neatly in the closet. Then I walked into the bathroom to assess the damage, feeling as though I was insulated from the world by a thick sheet of glass.

I'd washed my face at the station after they'd gotten some pictures of the damage, but I hadn't really looked at myself there. The woman in my mirror had dark purple moth-wing curves under her eyes and a flushed-red bruise on her face and looked as if she'd been dead for a week. My mind made the comparison before I realized it would be a long time before a joke like that would be funny again.

The ear the earring had been ripped out of was pink and smudged with blood, but not torn through. Small favors.

I washed my face again. The linen sheath would never look the same. I pulled it off carefully and hung it on a hanger over the showerhead. Dry clean only, the label said. I wondered if soaking it with photographic chemicals counted.

I'd put on my socks downtown; they stuck to the broken blisters now. I peeled them off carefully, but there was still a mess.

I washed my hands and my face again and peroxided the ear, putting a light silver post through it so the piercing wouldn't close while it healed. Just doing that made it start to bleed again, and the pale smears of blood made me want to weep. Shock. Sleep deprivation. Reality.

The phone rang.

There are very few people who phone me at eight in the morning. I picked up the receiver, glancing down at the phone. The answering machine tape was choked with incoming messages.

"Hello, Belle," I said. "I was right." Victory, as the poets say, is gall and wormwood.

There was a pause. "Bast?" Belle said. "Are you all right?"

I wondered what a truthful answer to that would be.

"I'm home now," I said unnecessarily.

"I tried to call you at the studio but I couldn't get through. I called Lieutenant Hodiac."

"Yeah, he came over and arrested Stuart."

I was so tired I was almost mumbling and the words came out with arrogant matter-of-factness. Apathy is the secret to sangfroid. "Look, I'm really zoned, so I'll call you tomorrow, okay?" I added. Tomorrow and tomorrow and tomorrow, but tomorrow never comes. Or is it another day?

"Do you want me to come down?" Belle said.

I realized with a pang of leave-taking that there would have been a time, once, when I would have wanted that, but not anymore. From her worldview to mine was finally too far to travel.

"No. I'll be fine. I'll call you. Thanks for asking."

"Take care of yourself, Bast," Belle said.

Sure. If not me, who?

There was Tsing-tao in the refrigerator and Slivovitz in the cupboard. I administered both, plus a long hot shower. I scrubbed until I looked like a boiled lobster, until vast tracts of skin were abraded and raw. I came out and put on my one surviving Banana Republic jumpsuit and padded around the apartment with my feet surgically swaddled in aseptic white socks. Everything hurt.

I wanted to go to bed, but I couldn't sleep while my apartment bore such witness to Stuart's presence. I shuffled around it like a zombie, putting things away, making things right, finding my shoes and earrings. Doing for myself what Ned had wanted me to do for him, a thousand years ago.

The two still-unreturned Books of Shadows I put on the kitchen table, along with the biography I'd borrowed from Daffydd.

Mary, Queen of Scots. Who drew everyone in her orbit into intrigue and violence. Whose influence did not stop with her death. Did Mad Maudlin haunt Elizabeth's bloody chamber down the long years as Elizabeth watched Mary's son—the rival's son who would be king thereafter while she herself was child-less—grow up across the border?

*For to see Mad Tom of Bedlam, ten thousand miles I'll travel / Mad Maudlin goes on dirty toes, for to save her shoes from gravel . . .*

Scotland's queen. Catholic or Witch—the Old Religion or the Oldest Religion? Always going home; never quite reaching it. Shadow queen and the proof—if it had been proof—gone once more.

*By a knight of ghosts and shadows, I summoned am to tourney / Ten leagues beyond the wild world's end, methinks it is no journey.*

Last of all I found the scattered pieces of my altar and assembled them again. It was almost noon, but I turned out my lights, lit my candles and incense, and petitioned my own Queen.

*Thank you, Lady, for keeping me alive. Now tell me what I'm going to tell . . . everyone.*

There was no answer. I hadn't expected any. I finished my beer, and snuffed the candles, and went to bed.

# 10

People who are fond of justice or sausages, to adapt a phrase, should never watch either being made. My testimony to the grand jury consisted of answers to questions that seemed meaningless; maybe they were parts of a pattern I wasn't privileged to see.

Mary, Queen of Scots, was not mentioned. Ned Skelton and Ilona Saunders were killed by Stuart Hepburn. Here's the proof. End of story.

And because this was so, my involvement in the actual trial—whenever it occurred—would probably be only as a footnote. Detective Larsen might have been right, and I wouldn't be called at all. Who wanted my unwelcome complications introduced into this particular passionless play?

Bail was set at the hearing, and Stuart Hepburn did not make bail. I wasn't there for that; ADA Morales, the assistant district attorney who had shepherded me through the case—and who would be prosecuting Stuart in the sweet bye-and-bye—called to tell me, which was kind of her. I felt a distant, dutiful sense of relief; while there was very little point in his killing me now that *The Book of Moons* was gone, I felt that Stuart was the sort to hold a grudge.

With one thing and another I didn't go back to Houston Graphics for two weeks, but I got reports. Houston achieved full employment through having to let the freelancers bill for cleaning up the mess Stuart had made. Ray finally convinced Mikey that whatever I'd done, I'd done while being held at gunpoint by a deranged killer. I kept my job.

And life went on, just as if Stuart had never been.

Julian got most of his stolen inventory back when Ilona's apartment in the back of Lothlorien (where Stuart had been staying) was searched. The insurance company was delighted.

Ilona's cat, which had also been staying at the apartment, was adopted by Glitter, a move that did not bode well for the future of Glitter's gold-lace curtains. She told me later its name was Yarrow. I did not make the obvious pun about a yarrowing experience. I didn't seem to have much sense of humor lately.

Belle was able to trace both Diana-27 and Otterleaf and get phone numbers for them. I used the Criss-Cross directory at New York Public and mailed their books back to them anonymously.

*Maria Stuarda* played all six of its performances to what Beaner said was critical acclaim. I didn't go to any of them. Beaner said he now considered that opera in the light thespians viewed "The Scottish Play" and hoped Goddess would strike him straight if he ever sang Robin Dudley again.

I returned *A Rose in the Shadows* to Daffydd. He'd heard about Stuart; by now, everyone had. He told me that Mary had frequently been accused of witchcraft in her lifetime, but that during the sixteenth century C.E. such an accusation had been about as much of a distinction as being called a godless Commie in the McCarthy era. If he'd heard of *The Book of Moons,* he didn't mention it.

Lothlorien closed.

I read, I slept, I took long walks. I talked to Ned and Ilona when they came to visit. I did some work at the Snake, I read tarot (gratis) at Chanter's Revel, I hung out. I did my best to come to terms with what Stuart had done to me. Beyond the slap, beyond the threats, beyond attempted murder.

Because of Stuart Hepburn, for the rest of my life I'd be sharing my life with a monster. A monster born out of fire, brittle and inflexible as volcanic glass, something that would live beneath my skin and would die or kill rather than live with being that afraid again. Something for which death held less terror than helplessness did; a monster that could seize control of my life at any moment and make me follow not my will, but its. Because of Stuart.

I visited Belle, more out of a sense of duty than anything else. She told me that hate would be a healthy reaction that I could work through, but I didn't feel anything I recognized as hate. I told her I thought I ought to take a sabbatical from Changing. We both knew what I really meant, but she didn't push me to make it formal.

I did a lot of ritual, I saw a lot of movies, and when the feeling that I needed to knock on my own door to make sure no one else was inside before going home was faint enough, I knew it was time to go back to work.

Monday, May 23, nine A.M. The day was overcast, hot and wet as a dog's breath. I got into the studio, doing my best impersonation of nonchalance. There was an almost full house of regulars, minus Royce. There was even a new hire, which was reassuring. Everything looked normal. We had a new coffeepot.

"Glad you finally decided you could make it," Ray said. He waved me over to his desk.

"Couldn't tear myself away." I came over and took charge of a dummy, spec sheet, and a folder full of type and photos. Virtue's reward. He'd saved it for me.

"You okay?" Ray said.

"Yeah, sure." Another inarticulate urban legend in the making.

I took the pile back to my carrel. Mikey was out on his rounds, so there was a certain amount of chatter. The official story, as current at Houston Graphics, seemed to be that I'd decided to work late at the studio and been surprised by a burglar. It was as good an explanation as any, and, best of all, did not involve Mary, Queen of Scots. I let it ride and accepted commiserations.

Tyrell thought I should carry a gun to prevent future incidents. Eloi spoke up enough to say that *he* never had any trouble (yeah, like somebody'd jump Bogie). Chantal said nothing like this ever happened in France, but it is Chantal's expressed opinion that all the evils of the Western World descend from the American insistence on using disposable grocery bags. Ray said that since I was going to sell my story for a Movie of the Week I'd become independently wealthy and could afford to hire a bodyguard.

Everybody's a comedian.

My work space had been carefully neatened by others to the point where I couldn't find anything. I spent the next ninety minutes putting everything back the way I wanted it. My coffee cup was missing its handle and would have to be replaced, but would do for today. I filled it with coffee and got to work as the studio settled down around me.

Royce got in around eleven. He was wearing a nice little houndstooth check that had last been seen in the Bogart/Bacall version of *The Big Sleep*. I hoped Eloi could contain himself.

I went back to work. A few minutes later I heard the sound of high heels. I looked up at Royce.

"Welcome back," he said. "This is yours, right?"

He held out a flat, brown-wrapped package. I felt all my cozy, self-congratulatory assurance vanish like water down a drain.

I took the package. On it was a red-and-white label of the kind the studio uses, and on it was typed: "M Q o S: B o M."

Mary, Queen of Scots: *Book of Moons*.

"Where?" I said, as if it were a complete sentence.

Royce looked embarrassed. "I hope you haven't been looking for it too hard," he said. "I took it home with a bunch of my stuff by mistake the day before the studio got tossed—it was out on the table. Ray said it didn't belong to Houston."

"Yeah—and stop using our wrapping paper on your personal jobs, Kitty," Ray called from the front. I waved fingers at him.

"No," I said, with what I hoped was conviction, "it wasn't anything I needed. Thanks, Royce."

He studied me closely, trying to decide if I was being completely truthful with him. Like me, Royce is also into what we frequently call "alternative spirituality," but as his path is the achievement of the Holy Grail he and I don't really have that much to talk about.

"Yeah, anytime. Don't get yourself into trouble, Bast," he said. He went back to his desk. I wish I had half the self-assurance in heels that Royce does.

I looked at the package. I took a mat knife and cut away a little corner of the wrapping, exposing the edge of an old leather book—the old leather book, in fact, that I'd expected to see. I set it aside, out of harm and spilled coffee's way.

I was not forced to revise my view of Stuart's intelligence or posit supernatural intervention after all. Stuart hadn't found *The Book of Moons* in the studio because it hadn't been here to find. Somehow it had managed to go home with Royce and safely absent itself from the events that followed.

Which might be supernatural intervention enough. I didn't, after all, remember leaving it out on a table, but that Tuesday's events were pretty hazy in my memory. I could have. Whether I had, in fact, was just one more thing I'd never know.

It took me eight weeks to copy out *The Book of Moons*—in modern ink on modern paper, creating something with no verifiable link to the past. I copied each word carefully, straining at the archaic Elizabethan "secretary hand," although I had little Latin and less French, and not much of the book seemed to be in English. Maybe someday I'd do a typescript version and get the whole thing translated.

And when I was done making my copy I swaddled the original in neutral pH tissue and placed it in the pale gray archival document box I had bought to store it in. I bound the box tightly in acid-free tape, and when I had wrapped *The Book of Moons* for the last time I took it up to the Pierpoint Morgan Library and told them I was a messenger with a parcel.

Parcels do get messengered, even to libraries. They let me in.

I'd used a blank from Lightfleet messengers, the service the studio uses; it wasn't hard to slip one out of Mikey's desk and mark it up, and I picked the day carefully. Rainy, and just an anonymous messenger's bad luck that the call sheet that would tell who it was from and who it was to was sodden beyond recognition. Maybe the Pierpoint Morgan'd come up with plausible answers on their own. God knew they'd get no answers from Lightfleet.

I left it in the hands of a bored receptionist who didn't seem to care whether or not it was ever delivered, let alone who I was. I tried not to care what happened now; I'd done what I could for Mary and her cause. The Pierpoint Morgan has one of the most extensive rare books collections outside the Vatican, as well as a nearly complete Visconti-Sforza tarot deck. They'd know what to do with a book that was very, very old. If it was, in fact, even that, and not some modern forgery.

Magic or not?, so the question goes, but the real question isn't, in the final analysis, what is there, but what we see. Reality is a consensus, arrived at through polling the testimony of individuals. Truth and reality are both in a constant state of mutation, and all anyone can do is ride the crest of his particular wave. Alone.

In the end, everyone's alone. It was the middle of the day in early August. I was on my lunch hour. I headed downtown, back to work.